In The Name of Love

Breanna J.

Author Breanna J. Presents In the name of the Love Copyright

ISBN-13: 978-1985833937

ISBN-10: 198583393X

Acknowledgements

First I want to thank my lord and savior Jesus Christ. Without him none of this would be possible. It's truly a blessing to know that he opened doors I never thought would be opened or an option for me. This book is nothing but god show off about the wonderful gifts he can give to us all. I will forever rejoice for the ways he has made for me.

Next I want to give honor to my Parents Vandell (Natasha) Marshall and Tamara Miller. Without them there would be no me. But most importantly I want to thank them for the values they have instilled into me. Without those values I would not be the creative, determined black queen I am today.

I can't mention my parents without giving my leading lady a shout out. Thank you to my grandmother Pamdora Dillard. For being the chief in our village. They say it takes a village to raise a kid and you kept that village going with a strong foundation for your kids, their kids, and possibly my kids.

To Bobby (Philipe) Cruz, Shan'Que Johnson, and Daniel Flowers thank you for always being there for me. No matter if I had writers block or need spell check you all were right there. You were my first ever readers and you gave me your honest option and feedback that prepared me for the world's. My love for you guys can be explained in words.

Then there's Chanda Duncan, my aunt and more importantly my best friend in the world. Thank you for always having that no option matters attitude. You were always there to be the voice of reason for me and pushing me when I was scared and wanted to give up.

To my high school teachers K. Yarnell and R. White. Thank you ladies for being mentors to me. You encouraged me to pick up a pen and express myself at some of the darkest times of my life. No one will ever know how much your kindness affected my life.

Finally last but not least, thank you to my readers. You guys make my dream a reality. I hope that my writing gives you that escape to let your imagination run wild.

BREANNA J.

Prologue

"Hello, I'm trying to surprise my husband Kendrick Shaw. Can you tell me what room he's in?" I asked the receptionist at the hotel as I slid a fifty dollar bill across the desk to her.

She swiftly took the fifty without making a scene and said, "Sure Mrs. Shaw, one moment. Mr. Shaw is on the 3rd floor in room 326. Here's the key. Enjoy your night, Mrs. Shaw."

"Thanks hun," I said with a smile as I walked over to the elevator.

I stepped into the elevator with a huge smile on my face and greeted the white couple in the elevator.

"Good evening."

On the inside, I was flipping out.

I thought to myself, *Sasha, what in the hell are you doing?*

I pushed the button for the 3rd floor and the elevator doors closed.

When the doors opened to the 3rd floor, I took a deep breath and stepped out. I stopped before walking towards the room and straightened myself. I made sure that the sexy silk

In The Name of Love

ankle-length trench coat I had on was straight and that the corset I had on under had my girls in the right spot.

Finally, I also patted my purse to make sure my gun was in reach if anything went wrong. Hopefully, I wouldn't have to use it because Lord knows I was scared of the kickback, but if I did need it, I wanted it close by.

I walked down the hall toward the room. When I got to the door, I stood to the right, so that when they cracked the door open, I would be able to still see into the room.

I took another deep breath and knocked.

A woman answered, "Who is it?"

"Housekeeping," I said back.

The woman opened the door and said, "The room is already clean, but we could use some more towels."

As she was talking, I could see Keyz in the corner of the room behind her pouring a drink in his boxers.

I pushed past the high yellow chick into the room.

"Bitch, move!" I said as I charged into the room, causing the door to hit her and knock her down.

I stood in the middle of the room and screamed, "Really, Kendrick?" as I threw a wine glass at the back of his head.

BREANNA J.

"Yo Keyz, this your Shorty?" he asked, smiling.

"Yes, that's my baby," Keyz answered.

"I'm nothing to you Keyz and you better explain what the fuck is going on and quick before I shoot you and his ass and be on the next episode of *Snapped*. Let's not forget I'm still on a thousand with you," I said to him with anger because I couldn't understand what type of twisted joke this was.

"Damn Keyz, your shorty is loyal. You're in the dog house and she was still willing to do a crime for you," the cop said.

Kendrick started laughing and responding to the cop as I walked off to my car.

I jumped back in my car and sped off. I was so pissed, but clearly, that was not on Kendrick's mind because he was not behind me driving home.

I pulled up in the driveway and parked my car in the garage. I walked into the house and dropped my purse on the living room couch. After I dropped my stuff, I went to the bar and poured myself a drink to ease my nerves.

As I finished the glass of Remy, I heard Kendrick coming in the house.

"Sasha, where the hell you at?" he yelled through the house.

I said nothing as I poured another glass of Remy and leaned against the bar, drinking it with an attitude.

IN THE NAME OF LOVE

He came charging into the dining room where the bar was.

"Sasha, what the fuck is wrong with you?" he asked me.

I looked at him with an attitude all over my face and responded.

"What the fuck is wrong with me? No, fuck you Kendrick, you don't get to ask me that. What the fuck is wrong with you? You're taking these bitches to hotels now. And good hotels at that. I mean I knew your ass was still cheating, but I didn't know you were out here tricking, too." I said as I pushed him in the forehead with my finger.

"Sasha baby, listen, it's not like that," he pleaded. "Yeah right muthafucka, you said that the last time. Your ass not even being smart with your shit. Are you even strapping up before you fuck these bitches? Never mind, don't answer with ya dirty ass," I said as I turned and walked towards the kitchen. "I should have cheated on your ass when I had the chance," I mumbled.

Kendrick walked up and grabbed my arm from behind.

"What the fuck you just say?" he asked me.

I looked him straight in the eyes and rolled my neck as I said, "You heard me. I should have cheated on you when I had the chance."

"Sasha, stop playing with me and watch your mouth. Cheat and get your ass killed. You know who I am," Kendrick said back to

BREANNA J.

me with his chest all poked out.

"Really, Kendrick? Me get killed? Ha! You kill me, I swear to God you do. Keyz's ass can cheat all he wants on Sasha, but Sasha is supposed to stay loyal and faithful to him while he's out there putting his dick any and everywhere. You got me all the way fucked up," I said to him.

"Sasha, I told you to chill. I told you it wasn't like that. I'm here with you, you're my woman. You are supposed to be faithful to me because I make sure you're good. Are you not taken care of? Do you have your dream home? Are you not living the life most bitches are dying to have?

So, why are you worried about these bitches? I don't love them. I love you. I might give them some dick here and there, but I'm telling them the truth. They know I got a wife that I go home to," Keyz pleaded with me

"Keyz, you're stupid," I said as I looked him in the eyes.

"No, you're stupid! You do too much, then you take the shit to another level and bring this out the house!" he said as he grabbed the gun off the couch that had fallen out my purse.

"Really? Kendrick? Really? Yes, I am well taken care of, but let's not get it twisted, I was well taken care of before you. Yes, I do have the dream home and the life I always wanted, but don't for one minute, get it twisted. The account that all the money come out of for this house and my dream life has my name on it, so don't think that it's solely you making this happen because without me, you would have never got connected when you moved down here. Without me, you'd have no way to clean your drug money. WITH-

In The Name of Love

OUT ME, YOUR WHOLE OPERATION WOULD BLOW UP IN YOUR FACE! I've put my time in to live this life here. I put my heart on the line. I clearly love your ass despite all the bullshit you do. So, understand this, this great life you say I have, I worked my ass off for and I am still working for," I told Keyz and began to walk into the kitchen again.

Then I stopped, "And as for the gun, that came with me for protection and I'm glad I did bring it since you mess with dummies that don't know their place. It's either that or you're just not telling these bitches their place and they feel like they can run up on me when I run up on your ass," I said to him.

Keyz walked up to me but with a different attitude this time.

"Well bae, you didn't have to hit the girl with the door when you rushed in the room nor did you have to hit her with the butt of your gun when you were leaving," he said to me in a sweet voice.

"Kendrick, you didn't have to be in the room then it would have been no issue. As a matter of fact, are you defending that hoe 'cause you can go be with that hoe if that the case. Last time I checked, I never asked you to follow me home. You could have stayed right there with her and nursed her back to health since you so worried about what I did to her," I said to him.

Kendrick smiled and started laughing.

"Baby, shut up. I don't care about that hoe."

I just looked at him because I don't think he understood how

BREANNA J.

serious I really was.

"I'm not laughing Kendrick, you don't care about me either," I said to him, fighting back tears.

"Baby I do care about you. Look, I'm going to wipe her blood off your gun for you. You would have gotten your ass caught because you were going to shoot a cop with this gun and it has blood on it."

I rolled my eyes.

"I wouldn't have gotten a charge for that girl because she's still alive. Since we are on the topic of the cop. who is he?"

"He's this cat named Tony I know from way back. I didn't even know he moved back here."

I walked off while Kendrick was talking. I didn't even desire anything out of the kitchen anymore. After all this, I was just ready to go to bed. I loved this man so much that I let him make a fool of me.

"I'm going to bed," I said while heading for the stairs.

"Okay, I'll be up there in a few minutes. I got some calls to make."

I stopped in mid-step.

"Nah, I'm good. You can sleep in the guest room or go run the streets like you normally do. As of right now, we aren't together," I said to Kendrick.

IN THE NAME OF LOVE

"Nah baby, I want to talk and show you that I am sorry for what I have been putting you through," he answered back.

I laughed and walked towards him.

"Keyz, baby, there is nothing in this world that would make me want to be in the same bed as you right now, let alone, engage in any making up you think is about to happen. You hurt me, and disrespected me *again*; so now this one, I don't even know if we will ever come back from. Only time can tell what is next for us, or if there will even be an us."

I turned and walked up the stairs.

For the first time in all the years that Keyz and I had been together, I said I was thinking about leaving him and I actually meant it.

I left Keyz standing at the bottom of the steps, looking broken and confused. Shit, he looked how I felt.

BREANNA J.

"What the hell happened?" I asked, concerned as I rushed over to look at Katrina's hand.

Katrina was still on 1000 and answered, "When I hung up with you, the bitch was still yelling, screaming, knocking over stuff and refusing to leave. I know you say that we are supposed to act professional at all times in the shop but this bitch took me there, Sasha. I got too tired of her, so I hit her and blacked out. When I came to, Keyz and Tasha was trying to get my hands from around the girl's neck. Once they got me to release her, Keyz dragged her out the shop. Two minutes later, Keyz was in front of the shop screaming "Fuck you" to the girl as she stuck her middle finger out her car window as she pulled off."

I apologized to Katrina over and over again. I felt so bad for her because Katrina was a hood chick that was really trying to change her life.

"Where is Keyz? "I asked them.

Tasha answered, "I believe he's in your office."

"Okay, y'all pull y'all self together. I am so sorry this happened to y'all. I will pay you guys for whatever clients you missed out on today," I said as I prepared to go to my office.

I walked off and headed to my office.

As soon as I opened the office door and got Keyz in my sight, I asked, "What the fuck is this, Kendrick?"

I slammed the door behind me.

In The Name of Love

"You got your bitches knowing where my business is now? I hope your ass knows that for every dime your little bitch cost me today your ass is covering. That includes the money my stylist missed out on today. You are going to pay it all."

Keyz interrupted me.

"SHUT UP SASHA, DAMN!" Keyz screamed out.

I jumped back because it was rare that he ever showed me this side of him.

"I know this is my fault, damn, I'm sorry I fucked up," Kendrick stated.

"Kendrick, you should have known better," I said as I pointed at him with tears in my eyes. "You know what Kendrick, I'm done. Go to the house and pack your stuff," I said as I walked towards the door.

"Sasha, come here," Kendrick said calmly

"Kendrick, I'm done, I'm leaving. Six years together and you didn't think to prevent this from happening? I hate…" I said as Kendrick interrupted me and blocked me from the door.

"Sasha, stop! Just listen and relax," he said, still in a calm voice as he leaned against the door so I couldn't open it.

"Sasha baby, I love you. You are my ride or die, my better half, the light when I was in my dark place of my life. I'm go-

BREANNA J.

Then, he began to eat my pussy like it was his last meal.

I leaned my head back and let out a sigh of pleasurable relief.

"Oh, my God," I moaned and bit my bottom lip.

He continued to eat my pussy like he was on a mission to find gold.

I sat my hand on the top of his head as a sign of encouragement that he had found the spot and to keep going right there. I looked down at this man and had so many flashbacks that made me shed a few tears. The same man that could make my body feel this great was the same man that continuously made my heart hurt. He was the same man that was once my best friend and now I felt like he was stranger that kept betraying my trust over and over again.

He kept going and so did the flashbacks of all the good times and the bad times, the late nights I spend up waiting for him to come home, the nudes and text messages I use to see in his phone, the laughs, and the romantic vacations.

A tear fell from my eye and my heart began to race.

"Oh my God, I'm about to cum," I said with tears in my eyes.

Kendrick kept going until I released.

He stood and leaned in for a kiss.

In The Name of Love

I turned my face and let him kiss my cheek.

He left out the office and went to the bathroom to clean his face.

I stood up and wiped my face and looked at myself in the mirror.

"This can't be my life. This won't be my life," I said to myself. "I am stronger than this. Kendrick knows better after all we been through, but it's all okay" I continued to say out loud to myself. "Since he doesn't love the woman I was for him, he will hate the bitch I will be towards him. That head he gave WAS NOT ENOUGH!"

BREANNA J.

Chapter Three

When Keyz returned from the bathroom leaning his face in the bathroom, he informed me that he had to go and make a few moves, but he would see me later on at the house. He left out the office. He must have been greeted by the mess in the salon because he turned back around and came back into the office.

"I'll call a cleaning company to come in and handle the damages out there. Also, go down to the bank and take out $1,000 from our joint account. Give that to Katrina and Tasha for the money they missed out on today," he said.

"Why do I have to go all the way down to the bank? Why can't you do it? This is all because of you anyway. Shit, you can't have one of your workers bring the money here out of the money we haven't cleaned yet? It's just a $1,000. That just means less that I have to take to the bank to be mixed in with the shop's money anyway," I sassed back to him.

"Sasha baby, please just do what I asked you, it will all work out in the end," he said as he gave me a forehead kiss.

His forehead kisses used to make me melt. It made me feel like he cared about me and as if I was the prettiest girl in the world. He would give me a forehead kiss before leaving the house or when I was going to bed. It made me feel like I was on his mind or like we had an emotional connection. Now that same forehead kiss did nothing for me. It was like it was a joke.

In The Name of Love

Once I straightened myself and my office up, I came out and sat at my station. I looked at the shop.

"Damn man," I said as I shook my head.

Never in a million years would I have thought that when CJ gave me the money for this place I'd ever have to go through this. I never thought that someone would destroy something I'd worked so hard to get up and running.

My salon was the one thing Keyz couldn't say he gave me or helped me get. This was a gift from my brother that I established and grew like it was my baby. I put my time in running this shop and making it what it was well before Keyz came in the picture. I had worked so hard showing that I could manage CJ's barbershop that when I asked him to fund my own salon, it was a simple yes. Not to mention, I could actually do hair.

Back then, I literally ran every part of the barbershop and made sure that the shop's money got to the bank on top of the money that CJ wanted cleaned.

CJ taught me so much that it was easy for me to help Keyz after CJ put him on.

In the years that Keyz and I had been together we had managed to gain rental properties, my brother's barbershop and a bar that we are waiting to open. But this, Elite Divas, was mine. If Keyz and I walked away from each other today, I would still have my salon.

The shop was the reason Keyz and I met back in 2008 be-

BREANNA J.

cause his cousin Latisha was working for me. She introduced Keyz to me and I remember sizing him up. For a down south 'Bama, baby had swag back then. He was sun kissed and that chocolate smooth skin glowed in such a sexy way. He stood six feet tall with muscles that made me envision him carrying me. He had dreads that he always kept pulled back in a po-nytail. When he smiled at me and I saw his prefect smile and dimples, I was hooked.

I knew for sure I would never give him the time of day. His appearance let me know he was a pretty boy. After being around my brother and his boys, I knew that pretty boys didn't bring anything but drama to your life. It was everything from the girls to them just feeling themselves I knew that wasn't what I wanted in my life. I was still stuck on myself and be-ing the center of attention. I mean, I was 5'5" with the perfect body and full lips. I had a head full of beautiful natural hair and Hershey toned skin. Guys told me I had brown eyes that pulled you in.

Keyz flirted with me every chance he got no matter how much I tried to ignore him and act uninterested. When he came in for his dread retwist, he would compliment me and spit major game, but I knew Keyz had mad bitches. He had bitches from here on his dick just because he was a pretty boy from out of town and there was no telling what bitches he had back where he was from.

One day during his appointment, he asked me out on a date. I had been single for a few years because CJ would run off any dude that tried to talk to me, so I agreed. I mean, in my head even if the date was wack, it was a reason to get dressed up and show that I still had it.

In The Name of Love

I told him I would meet him at the restaurant. He joked and asked why he couldn't pick me up. He asked did I think he was going to kidnap me.

My smart mouth answered back, "Maybe."

He told me to meet him at LeBernardin which was some shit I had never even heard of before, but I agreed. That night I went home and Googled the restaurant online. I needed to figure out how I should dress. The restaurant looked so luxurious in the pictures, so I knew I had to come correct.

I stood in my closet for thirty minutes throwing stuff around. CJ came home and asked what I was doing. I brushed him off and told him I was getting ready for a night out with the ladies, so he left me alone.

I pulled out this long black dress I had been dying to wear. It was spaghetti strapped, showed a little side boob with a low cut back that stopped right above the crack of my ass and a split that came up half my thighs. I dressed it up with a gold rhinestone bracelet, gold dangly earring and some all black open toe heels.

Then I sat at my vanity and straightened my hair. Keyz was used to seeing me in my everyday clothes at the shop, so I wanted to do something different. I did my makeup; it was simple but I made sure it enhanced my good features.

I got dressed. After I finished, I stood in the mirror and admired myself. It had been a while since I was able to get this dressed up.

BREANNA J.

As I looked my appearance over in the mirror Keyz called to tell me he was leaving his house, heading to the restaurant. I told him okay and that I was leaving my home as while, but I actually didn't leave the house for another ten minutes.

I wanted Keyz to already be there and waiting for me. That way when I pulled up he could admire my fine ass.

When I arrived, Keyz was waiting outside for me. The boy was dressed to impress. He actually shocked me. I was expecting hood nigga attire like I normally saw him in. He had on an all-black suit that properly fit him. He had a white shirt underneath that was open just enough to see a little bit of his chest. He wore black dress shoes and a watch that sparkled as much as my lip gloss. His dreads were pulled back in a bun.

When he greeted me with a hug, he smelled so good that if I had on panties that night, they would have been soaked.

As we entered the restaurant, he opened every door for me and pulled out and pushed in my chair. He was being such a gentlemen. This date was going so much better than I ever expected. He was definitely getting brownie points for being so much more than the average hood nigga I thought he was.

We held a great conversation all night. The man had so much knowledge and wisdom. I felt bad that I had prejudged him before I got to know him. After we left dinner, neither of us were ready to go home. We were both having such a great time. We decided to go to Paley Park. We talked some

In The Name of Love

more and laughed. We even shared our first kiss in front of the waterfalls. The night was nothing less than a scene from a movie.

What the hell happened to us? Reminiscing on that night made me so confused on how we got here. I mean after that night me and Keyz couldn't be separated. He would bring me flowers just because. He would take me on dates. He even sat up with me some nights on the phone until God knows when.

When we finally became a couple and I introduced him to CJ, they hit it off. I knew it was meant to be. He treated me great and he and my brother got along. What more could a girl want?

I never would have thought that years later Keyz would be running around acting like King of the fuck boys and CJ would be dead.

At this point, all I knew was that I was tired. Tired of feeling alone and wanting my brother back. Tired of having unanswered questions. Tired of the way Keyz was treating me. Tired of going back and forth with him just to end up still being with him. I was tired of his games and lies.

I was so tired of where I was in life right now that I had stopped going to church because I felt like I was praying and it wasn't working. I was at a breaking point. I couldn't even cry any more about the stuff life was putting me through. All I could do now and days was hear CJ in my head saying, "You're a soldier and you do not give up."

BREANNA J.

So every day I got up and put a smile on my face and I fought for my relationship with my man. I had to be honest. I was running out of hope and ideas to keep me and Keyz going.

As I sat at my station thinking, I heard the shop door open.

"Sorry we're closed," I said while looking in the mirror.

"Sasha Brown?" the voice called from behind me.

"Yes, that's me," I said as I turned around in the chair towards the unknown guest.

When my eyes locked on the guest my heart dropped.

"Oh my God, it's you! Tony, let me explain. I didn't mean to pull that gun on you. I was just…" I pleaded.

"Sasha, calm down! It's water under the bridge. I see Kendrick told you who I am," Tony said.

"Yes, he told me who you are. If you aren't here about last night, what are you here for because Keyz is not here? As a matter of fact, how do you know my full name or where my business was located?"

Tony smirked at me.

"Sasha relax honey, I've known Keyz for a while so after me and him were done talking last night, I took his plate number down. I ran it through my system and just like I thought

IN THE NAME OF LOVE

the car was registered in your name. From there, I did a little research to find out that the lovely Ms. Sasha Brown wasn't only a loyal rider to her man but a successful business owner and landlord."

I looked at Tony.

"That's all nice, but why are you here then?" I asked with an attitude.

Tony answered, "Well, I seen that you were really upset when you pulled off so I wanted to check up on you and make sure you were okay."

I looked at Tony up and down.

"Yes, I'm great, thanks. Keyz and I are great. I'll make sure to let him know you came by."

"You don't have to tell him; it's not that serious. Ummm, is everything okay here? It looks like a burglary," he said to me.

"Everything is fine; my *man* is handling it," I told me.

Tony smiled and handed me his business card.

"Alright then, you enjoy the rest of your day, Ms. Brown," Tony said as he exited the shop.

BREANNA J.

Chapter Four

As Tony walked out the salon I couldn't help but stare and wonder why this man went out his way to find little old me. I didn't notice it last night, but Tony as was so fine and that's probably because I couldn't see past the uniform he had on.

Tony was dark skinned, just like Keyz. His face was so gentle though. He rocked a brush cut with a part on the side. Unlike most of the men that was following the trend, he didn't have a beard, but he had a goatee that was neat and lined up. With the quarter length sleeve shirt he had on, I could see that at least one of his arm had tattoos on it.

Damn! Maybe that was what I needed, a legal man with a government job. He would probably treat me right. He'd value the queen I was. He would be supportive and we could speak positivity into each other while being each other's number one fan. He probably wouldn't hide stuff from me or have a problem properly communicating. I would probably never have to worry about where he was or when he was coming home because he would always keep me informed on what was going on with him.

He would be passionate about me, us and where we were growing to. He would be someone I could sit and laugh with, cry with and be completely myself with. Someone that would make me feel more confident then I already was because they uplifted me. Who was I fooling? I loved Keyz's ass down to his damn dirty underwear and I wasn't giving up on what we had. I couldn't; I had invest so much already. I

IN THE NAME OF LOVE

couldn't let another woman be the defeat that sent me into the arms of another man. Hell, it be the defeat that sent me into the arm of one of Keyz's friends. I was better than that. Not to mention that wouldn't resolve anything.

It would just make me look like a hoe in Keys eyes no matter how many times he had cheating on me. He would never get over the fact that I hurt him. Normal nigga shit. Guys could dish it out, but when you do to them what they had been doing to you, shit, it turned into World War Five.

"Sasha!" I spun around and saw Katrina and Tasha standing there looking at me.

"What are y'all still doing here?" I asked them, shocked.

"Nah heffa, the question is what is going on here?" Katrina asked.

I tried to laugh off the question.

"Girl, nothing."

They both looked at me.

"No for real Sasha, what's going on? Bitches coming in here breaking up the shop and fine men coming in here looking for you," Tasha said.

"And did I hear you say you pulled a gun on that fine ass man?" Katrina asked.

We all laughed.

BREANNA J.

"Y'all, its nothing for y'all to worry about. I got everything under control."

Tasha walked up to me.

"Sasha, we are family, you can tell us what is going on. We are not here to judge you."

Katrina added, "Yeah, we just want to help you and find out if your new fine friend got some fine friends for your friends."

We all laughed again.

"Well, the bitch that fucked up the shop is one of Keyz's hoes. I caught them together in the hotel last night." I said.

"What the fuck, man! Let me take my seat," Katrina said.

"So, last night I was at home budgeting our check book like I normally do on Monday night and I go to refresh the bank website. When it refreshed, a new charge for the Marriott downtown popped up, so before I called the bank and cursed and screamed about wrongful charges, I called Keyz," I told them and then took a deep breath.

"I called the first time and got no answer. I waited a little while and called again. Once again, I got no answer. By this time, I was completely flipping out at home and I called again. There was still no answer. So, I said fuck it. I was going up there to see who had a room. I got dressed and put on some lingerie and a trench coat."

IN THE NAME OF LOVE

Tasha interrupted me, "What the fuck was the lingerie for?"

"Well, I figured that if he was cheating, I was free enough to kick some ass and if he wasn't cheating, I was sexy enough to distract him from my crazy ways," I told them.

"Okay, so what happened when you got to the hotel?" Katrina asked.

"Basically, long story short, bitch, I was Faith Evans in Notorious. I knocked on the door. The bitch opened it and Keyz was in his boxers preparing a drink. I pushed past that bitch and flipped out on his ass. The chick wasn't even my focus. She didn't owe me no loyalty, he did, but that bitch wanted to get crazy and grab on me. So, I popped that bitch in the head with my gun like "Here bitch, you should of had a V-8."

The girls burst out laughing.

"Yo Sasha, you bugged out!" Tasha said.

"Just a little bit," I said with a smile.

"So, Shorty that fucked up the shop today was Shorty from last night?" Katrina asked.

"Yup," I shrugged.

"Damn, so you tapped that ass last night and Kat did it this morning," Tasha laughed.

BREANNA J.

"Okay but who was the cutie that just walked out of here?" Katrina asked.

"That's Officer Tony," I said.

"Officer? Shit, he can arrest me anytime. Hell, my license suspended is right now!" Katrina said.

"Oh my God, you're so stupid, girl. I pulled a gun out on Officer Hottie last night," I said.

"What the fuck," they both said.

"So, after I left the hotel I was racing home and Keyz was following. Tony pulled him over. I got nervous because I didn't know if Keyz had drugs in the car. He had beat that other drug charge by the skin of his teeth two years ago, so I bust I U turn and got behind them. When the cop had his back to me, I pulled my gun on him," I explained to them.

As I said it, I heard how dumb I sounded.

"Hold the fuck up now! I got to be a real friend and keep it honest with your ass. Bitch, you pulled a gun on a cop for a nigga that you just found cheating on you less than an hour before! Are you fucking stupid? Now, I have silently watched you do a lot of dumb shit over this man and I didn't say nothing because I figured the dick was good, but this? That by far was the stupidest thing I have ever heard come out of your mouth. You could have gone to jail or worse gotten yourself shot. You know these cops don't give a fuck! They pull the trigger and then act innocent later," Katrina said as Tasha sat there nodding her head in agreeance.

IN THE NAME OF LOVE

I sat and listened to ever word Katrina said because honestly I needed to hear it.

"Bitch, enough is enough. Keyz has been doing his dirt for too long. When are you going to let his ass go? You're not an ugly girl, so you can get another nigga and you're not broke, so you don't need his money," Tasha said to me.

"Like, look at the last 24 hours. His intentions put you in danger of going to jail or being killed. He got your shop destroyed and fucked up our money and I don't like my money played with," Katrina said.

I sat there with tears rolling down my face.

"Sasha, we love you. We aren't trying to make you cry," Tasha said as she walked over and hugged me and Katrina followed.

I wiped my face and said, "I know, and thanks guys for being there for me."

They both smiled at me.

"That's what friend are for," Tasha said. "Friends? Bitch, we're family and that's what family does for each other," she said.

I stood up and took a deep breath. I looked around. I looked at these two ladies that were standing before me ready to ride with whatever I said I was going to do at this point just because they truly loved me.

BREANNA J.

We all gathered our belongings to close up the shop until it was cleaned up.

As we stood outside and I locked the doors to my baby, Katrina asked me.

"So Sasha, what are you going to do?"

IN THE NAME OF LOVE

Chapter Five

I stood there with a look of confusion. There was so many things I had to think about. Why was I going through all of this? Do I tell Keyz his mans came up to the shop and was running our info? Or should I mind my business and let them niggas handle that shit when it comes to the light? And what do I do about Keyz? His dirt had followed me all the way to my place of business and that was not acceptable.

I got to the car and sat there in the driver seat. There was no destination in mind, but I knew for sure I didn't want to go home. There were times like this where I only wanted one person to be around.

I put the car in drive and pulled off from the shop. I drove and drove. Before I knew it, I was at the cemetery that CJ was buried in.

I hadn't been here since our final goodbye two years ago, so I wasn't sure what made me come here. Since I was here, I figured I'd get out and walk over to his site.

As I got closer and closer to his grave my throat started to feel dry and my hands were shaking. When I got there, I kneeled down and rubbed the picture of my brother that was on the head stone. I cleared off all the leaves from around his headstone and took a seat.

A tear rolled down my cheek when I thought about that day when I laid my brother to rest. I missed his voice and just him being around him. He always gave me the best advice.

BREANNA J.

He was the best big brother a girl could ask for. He was a protector, a provider, caregiver and so much more. Now being without him was just so hard.

Even before our mom passed, it was always just us two. It was always CJ and Sasha, ride or die until the death of us. I had squared up with the toughest chicks over my brother with no questions asked and my brother had knocked out multiple niggas that thought they were going to treat me like anything less than a queen.

I still remember the first time CJ had to man up and take care of me. My mom left us home alone for three days with no food and no clue whether when or if she was back. She was out tricking and getting high. At this point, we didn't even hold her addiction against her or even go looking for her anymore. She was the drugs and the drugs were her. Honestly, her being on them and gone was easier to deal with then her when she was coming down from her high and needed her next fix.

My mom's issue taught CJ and I how to hustle. CJ went to the store and stole us chips and any other snacks he could get his hands on. He vowed that would be the last time we would have to struggle just to eat. He was so protective of me even at a young age that he made sure I was full and tucked me into bed at night before he took a bite of anything.

The next morning when all the drug dealers hit the block, CJ had me up, dressed and outside. He was convinced that he was going to talk to this guy that went by Snake. He was the drug king in our neighborhood. CJ wanted Snake to put him on.

IN THE NAME OF LOVE

CJ walked up to Snake holding my hand and told him he was ready to work and to put him on. At first, Snake laughed, but when he looked and saw how serious CJ was, his face changed. He asked what he needed that made him want to step into a grown man's business so early.

CJ told him with a straight face, "I got to feed me and my sister, and if you don't put me on, I will just go to another hood searching for someone to put me on until I get a yes."

Snake let him know that the drug world was a dog eat dog world. CJ didn't care. He told him he would do whatever to make sure that we were good.

From that day on, CJ was a dope boy. By the time our mom came back home three or four days later, CJ had made enough money to put groceries in the house and pay the light bill. After that, anytime my mom left us it didn't even matter to us. We were not even bothered by her absence. CJ was grinding, taking care of home and stashing money away. No matter how much CJ got tied up in the street, he refused to let me get tied up in them, too.

He made sure every day that I got to school and that no one ever knew that our mom was absent and out there on drugs. CJ was my protector and he was doing whatever was possible to keep CPS or anyone else from bothering us.

Not a day goes by that I don't wish he was still here to protect me like that. Even once we were completely grown, we were still a unit. CJ got close to Snake and became his right hand man. Snake eventually showed him the ropes as far how to run the business, and when Snake got locked up, CJ

BREANNA J.

became the head nigga in charge.

By that time, I was slaying hair out of our apartment. I had all the chicks in the hood on point. I was making enough money to not have to ask CJ for everything.

I remember one night I was coming from doing hair for one of the older ladies in the hood that didn't leave her house and some young niggas tried to rob me.

It wasn't the first time I had seen a gun, but it was the first time I seen one pointed at me. I suddenly felt the fear of not knowing what could happen next.

The dude must have gotten a got a good look at my face because he asked me, "Aren't you Calvin Jr's little sister?"

"His name is CJ, and yes I am," I said, mad at the current situation.

Calling CJ Calvin Jr was disrespectful to him. After our dad left us and our mom for a white woman and a better future, CJ vowed that anything to do with Calvin Sr he wanted nothing to do with, even the name.

Needless to say that when the guy realized who I was he begged for forgiveness and pleaded for me not to tell my brother. It was something about our bond that even when CJ wasn't physically there, he was still protecting me. I let that guy live and I didn't tell my brother, but after that night, I made it my business to buy my own gun so I could handle my own.

In The Name of Love

I laid on my brother's grave and imagined the days when we were kids and I would get scared and cry in bed; CJ would come in my room and hold me and let me lay on his chest until I fell asleep.

Keyz used to make me feel protected like that, but I don't know what happened. Now and days, he was an entire different man.

As I laid there remembering my brother, my peace was interrupted with a phone call. I tried to clear my voice as I answered the phone.

"Hello," I answered with a sound of annoyance in my voice.

"Sasha, you good?" Keyz asked.

"Yes, I am fine, what do you want?" I asked him angrily.

"I was just calling to check on you bae. I wanted to see what you were doing and where you were," he said back.

I took a deep breath and said, "I'm talking to CJ."

"What the fuck, Sasha? Stop playing! What are you doing for real and where are you?" Kendrick asked with an angry tone in his voice.

"Kendrick, I am at the cemetery visiting CJ."

I rolled my eyes.

Breanna J.

"Oh okay baby, why didn't you just say that the first time? You said you were talking to him like you were losing your damn mind," Keyz laughed, as if he had said something funny.

I rolled my eyes again.

"Kendrick, what do you want?" I asked once more.

"I was trying to see when you were going to be home."

"I will be there when I get there," Sasha answered.

"Well, make it soon. I got something I want you to do with me."

"Yup."

Click.

I pulled myself together and walked towards my car. Leaving the cemetery reminded me why I didn't come up here. It felt like I was leaving CJ all over again. It was hard to come to terms with the fact I was the only person I had now. Daddy had been gone since I was five. My mom and brother were both dead. And now I was with Keyz, who was being retarded.

I had been fighting so hard for me and Keyz just so I didn't have to be in this cold world alone, but this battle of drugs and money had defeated my mom and CJ. Ultimately, it caused me to be alone. Now my household was losing a battle between money and lust. I honestly feared that the same thing

IN THE NAME OF LOVE

was going to happen.

I hopped in my car and decided to drive through my old hood. Sometimes I would drive through there just to remember where I came from and why I was who I was. This hood had made me a soldier, a survivor, a hustler, and a fighter. Other than that, it had shined light on the things I no longer wanted to be a part of and the hurt that should have destroyed me at a young age.

BREANNA J.

Chapter Six

I stopped at the red light at the corner of the street we use to live on. It seemed like everything was the same. Things were moving just the same with a few new and younger faces because the old heads were out the game, dead or in jail.

As I sat at the light, I heard someone yell my name. I looked around and spotted P-nut. When the light turned green, I pulled over and P-nut walked up to the car.

P-nut was one of the dudes that used to sell for CJ once he took over the game. I hadn't seen him or any of the people that worked for my brother since he had passed away.

"Yo girl, what's up? What you are doing in this neck of the woods?" he asked as he walked over to the car.

"I'm good Nut, how the streets treating you?" I asked as he got closer to the car.

"I'm still eating lovely, thanks to your man. Had it not been for him we all would have been starving out here when CJ died," P-nut said.

I looked a little confused at him.

Really? I thought to myself.

I thought he was only in control of that area my brother gave him back when he was alive.

In The Name of Love

"Yea, Keyz has been making sure we get that package every week for the last two years. He hasn't missed a beat," he continued. "He sends Pookie down here to make sure that we are good. He collects the money and does the deliveries. We don't even see Keyz no more, but word on the street is he is trying to expand and get some more territory so we can make some more money. You know I am always down for more money," P-Nut said with a smile.

Now my mind was racing, even Keyz's best friend Sean was in on this shit, too.

Ain't that some shit.

This nigga was always at my house eating up our groceries and calling me sis, but for the last two years he had been in on this damn secret. I guess the bro code will always overrule right and wrong.

P-nut kept talking and telling me about all the stuff going on in the community.

I noticed a young girl stumbling out one of the public assistance apartment buildings. She was crying. Normally, I didn't pay these bitches in the hood any attention, but this girl had my attention because she looked so much like my mom.

I had to take a double look. It was as I were seeing my mom back in her prime before the drugs. I was looking at Alicia when she was sexy and a force to be reckoned with. That was back when every nigga wanted her but my dad had her. The girl had jet black hair down to her mid back, caramel brown skin and hazel eyes with a Coca-Cola bottle shape.

BREANNA J.

I tried to ignore her, but my heart wouldn't let me.

In the middle of P-nut talking, I jumped out the car.

"Sasha, where are you go?" he yelled as I walked towards the girl.

She was now sitting on the curb.

"Nut, I'll be right back," I said as I waved him off.

"Man Sasha, leave that water head hoe alone!" P-nut responded.

"P-nut, shut the fuck up and watch my damn car!" I said.

I walked up to the girl and handed her a napkin I had brought out of the car with me.

I felt like I had a knot in my throat and I couldn't speak. Being close to her was like reliving happy memories. I took a deep breath and squatted down.

"Here, honey."

She looked up at me. Her makeup was running and the look in her eyes screamed, "Save me."

She looked heart broken and alone. I could tell she was young because she had a baby face, but her eyes spoke that the world was getting the best of her.

"Are you okay?" I asked her.

IN THE NAME OF LOVE

She looked at me and asked, "Would I be stupid if I told you I'm not sure?"

Her response was so understandable to me because it was something my mom use to say to me when she was coming down off her high and I would check on her. Not to mention that at this point in my life I wasn't sure if I was okay, either.

I looked at her and said, "Nope, you wouldn't sound stupid at all; you would sound honest."

I reached my hand out to help her off the curb.

When she stood up, I introduced myself.

"I'm Sasha. What your name?"

"I'm Kimberly, but they call me Hazelnut," she told me.

The nickname let me know that either she was a stripper or a hoe, which would explain why she was half dressed in the middle of the day.

"Well, I'ma call you Kim because I don't want to know the street you," I told her.

She smiled.

I could tell it had been a while since someone was genuinely nice to her.

"Kim, come take a ride with me," I said as I walked to my car.

BREANNA J.

She looked at me, confused.

"Where are we going?" she asked.

I looked at her.

Honestly, I didn't know. Something in my heart just wouldn't let me leave her here, so I was following my gut.

"Let go eat, it's on me," I said.

She put a pep in her step.

"Well, in that case, sure."

We walked over to my car and got in.

P-nut leaned into my window and said, "Sash', why you trying to be super save-a-hoe?"

I mean mugged him.

"P-nut, shut the fuck up! You talk too damn much with your simple ass," I said as I pulled off, almost running over his foot.

As we drove, Kim told me she was only 18. She had lost her mom almost a year ago. Like most kids in the hood, she didn't know her dad and was therefore left alone once her mom died in a drive by shooting. She told me that she was making her way day to day. She avoided the system because she had turned 18 two months after her mom passed.

In The Name of Love

I asked her where she wanted to get a bite to eat.

She answered, "I'm okay with McDonalds. We can go through the drive-thru that way noone sees you with me."

I told her no problem but that I wasn't worried about who seen me. I drove to the nearest McDonalds and let her order whatever she desired. While she ate, I parked in an empty lot and we talked.

She told me had got a job at Classy Cuts, a local strip club to take care of herself. She said at first she was doing it so she can go to school during the day because it was her senior year, but she told me to make enough money she gave up school a few weeks ago. Knowing that she dropped out so close to finishing crushed me. Senior year was supposed to be the best time because there was prom, senior trips, and figuring out what you were going to do for the rest of your life.

I asked her where she was living and she told me that some nights she was staying in the dressing room at the strip club and other night she was letting guys take her home with them just so she could sleep in a bed.

Kim's story broke my heart. She was so young and had to experience some of the hardest things in life all by herself. She was such a beautiful girl and shouldn't be turning tricks just to survive. When I was her age, I was the hood princess and I had no worries. It reminded me of how good I had it because someone cared enough about me to make sure I didn't have to worry. My brother was the kingpin that made us seem like royalty and untouchable. The only things I was worried about was what I was wearing to prom and getting the latest

BREANNA J.

everything.

When she finished eating, I drove around.

Kim dosed off for a second and I just looked at her. I couldn't take this girl back to the hood and leave her. So, I kept following my gut. I was going to take her under my wing and help her.

I pulled up to the extended stay hotel that was around the corner from my salon.

"Hey Kim, wake up."

I shook her.

She opened her eyes and looked around.

"Why are we here?" she asked.

"This is where you are staying tonight," I told her.

Kim said, "Okay, no problem. Just let me fix myself up before you bring the guy in."

I looked at her.

"No, honey. No, it will be none of that tonight or ever again if I can help it."

I walked in and checked her into a room. I took her to the gift shop to get some hygiene products and stuff that she may need for the night.

IN THE NAME OF LOVE

Once she got everything she needed, we went up to her room.

I checked the room out to make sure everything was okay and that she would be safe. I put $50 on the nightstand and told her to use it if she got hungry.

Kim looked around the room in amazement.

"Okay Kim, I'm leaving. I'll be back at like 10 AM; we look like we are the same size, so I'm sure I have something in my closet that I'm no longer wearing that I can bring you tomorrow. Then you can go to work with me at my shop."

Kim ran to me and hugged me tightly. She began crying.

"Oh my God, Ms. Sasha! Thank you so much. I don't know why you are doing all this for me, but I appreciate it."

It had been so long since someone had hugged me like this. It made me feel loved. That was the way I felt when my and CJ used to embrace each other.

BREANNA J.

Chapter Seven

I got to my car and closed the door. I cried right in front of the hotel.

"Lord, I'm not sure what you're trying to show to me through this girl, but I am listening and obeying," I said out loud.

I wiped my face and pulled off. I drove home thinking of everything that had happened today from the sad news about my shop being destroyed to finding Kim.

Even the conversation with P-nut kept playing back in my mind. In two years, Keyz had never once said he had taken over all of my brother's areas. There definitely wasn't a change in our bank accounts. So, where was this extra money he was now making?

I pulled up to my home and took a deep breath when I saw Keyz's car and bike parked in the driveway.

"Damn, he's here," I said out loud with an attitude.

I got out the car and walked in the house. There were candles lit all over the place and 90s slow jams softly playing.

Does he think this is an enough? I thought to myself. *It's going to take more than a romantic set up to make up for the hell he has put me through.*

In my mind Keyz was a cheater, a liar, and now

In The Name of Love

couldn't even be trusted business wise. The cheating I could have probably gotten over if it wasn't a mistake he kept making, but when we start adding on the lies and secrets about a business I helped him make a success, that was an issue. Now I could understand why no matter how many legal ventures I put in front of him, including rental properties and the bar, he still decided to be in the streets.

I walked through the house, but there was no sign of Keyz.

I went in the den and looked through today's mail. I wanted to see whether Keyz was getting mail from another bank. I just never noticed and I needed to know where the hell this extra money was that this nigga was hiding. And, the question was why was he hiding money? I never asked his ass for shit. I made my own money. Shit, I was always giving him ideas to make more money. I searched and searched but couldn't find anything.

I heard Keyz talking loudly on the phone in the basement so I figured my search would have to happen another time.

I refused to participate in this romantic shit with this liar so I went upstairs and laid across the bed and closed my eyes. I just wanted to put my mind to rest. Twenty minutes or so went by and I dozed off.

Keyz must have come upstairs from the basement and realized my car was there. I could hear him going through the house calling my name, but I didn't bother to answer.

He came upstairs and opened the room's door.

BREANNA J.

"Sash?" he called.

I was awake and could hear him, but I didn't even bother to move. I kept my back towards the door and pretended I was sleep. In my head, I figured if I pretended I was sleep, he would just leave me alone. My effort was null and void. He kneeled on the bed and shook me.

"Bae, wake up," he said.

I rolled over and faced him.

"Damn Keyz, what do you want?" I asked in a sleepy voice.

He looked at me.

"When the hell did you get home?" he asked.

"Keyz, I been here for maybe an hour or so," I told him.

"So, why didn't you come find me?" he asked.

I barked at him with an attitude.

"Kendrick, I'm tired; today has been a hell of a day and I'm ready to put it to an end. The candles and shit is a nice gesture but..."

Keyz interrupted me and raised his voice, "Sasha, get the fuck up yo and come downstairs so we can talk!" he yelled.

I sat up on the side of the bed and looked at him.

In The Name of Love

"Okay, you want to talk? Fine, let talk," I said.

We walked downstairs.

When we got to the living room, I sat on the couch and said, "Now, let's talk because I got questions."

Keyz said, "Before we do all that, come with me."

I rolled my eyes.

"Keyz, you said come downstairs so we can talk, so here I am and I'm ready to talk," I said to him loudly.

"Sasha, just listen to me, damn!" he said back.

"I'm listening; your ass is just not saying anything I want to hear," I snapped back.

"Sasha!" he yelled.

I looked at him for a few minutes. Then, I got off the couch and followed him to the back door. He opened the door and I stepped out on to the back porch. The view was beautiful. There was a table on the back porch set up for a candlelight dinner.

I was so moved, but I couldn't let him see that. He had never gone to this extreme before.

Keyz came out the house and handed me a glass of wine.

BREANNA J.

"Give me your hand, I want to show you something," Keyz said.

I wasn't sure what else he was going to show me. I could see the table clear as day.

He walked me to the end of the porch and I looked out into the backyard to see candles in the shape of a heart. The middle was filled with rose petals spelling out I'm sorry. I started crying. I couldn't hold back the tears.

Keyz led me out to the yard and to the middle of the heart. There was a box waiting.

"Open it," he said from behind me.

I looked at him confused. I turned around and leaned down. I pulled the tabs on the box to open it. Three balloons popped out the box. Each balloon had one word on it. The first balloon read, "Will," the second read, "You," and the last had three dots.

I was confused.

As I turned to Kendrick, I asked, "Will I what?"

When I turned around completely, I saw that Kendrick was down on one knee. I covered my mouth with my hands. This couldn't be what I thought it was.

"Sasha Marie Brown, will you marry me?" he asked.

I stood there in disbelief.

In The Name of Love

"Sasha? I know we have been together for years. I know I have hurt you, but after seeing the hurt in your eyes last night, and again today, I knew I had to do better. With this ring, I promise to you to be better man for you and only you," he explained.

After all these years, this man had finally asked me to marry me. It was crazy that on the oddest day of my life, I got this question. I couldn't believe we were here and he was asking this. I couldn't deny that I was happy. I loved him no matter what, but I still couldn't help but wonder whether this was enough. Is this right? Why now? Does this change anything? Is this real?

"Sasha?" Keyz said again.

"Yes, yes, I will marry you," I blurted out.

Keyz stood up and hugged me. We kissed.

After the embrace, we went back to the porch and the table that Keyz had set up for us.

As we ate dinner, I continued to look down at my hand.

Keyz peeped my look and asked, "What's wrong, baby? Do you not like the ring? We can pick you out another one if you don't like it."

I looked at him and said, "No it's beautiful, but Keyz, what made you do this now?"

Keyz took a deep breath and looked me in the eyes.

BREANNA J.

"Honestly, I had been thinking about it for a while but I was being selfish. I wasn't ready to give up my ways, but today, it finally hit me and I put my nerves aside. I realized that if I didn't make a major change for you I was going to lose you. And I know there is no other woman out there that's going to love me the way you do. So, why not give you all of me and everything else you deserve."

I smiled and blushed at the same time. He hadn't talked like this to me in a while.

"Nah, you seen what I did to your little side chick and didn't want me to do that to you," I said to him.

We both laughed.

"Girl, ain't nobody worried about you and that gun. I always knew you were the one, ever since the first day I saw you. I love everything about you. The way you walk, talk, that beautiful smile, and even your mad face. You push me to be better. You speak to me in a way no one else does. You put your heart in my hands a while ago and it's finally time I do right with it. I'm the only family you got, so why not make it official from here on out that I'm all about you," he said as he held my hands.

We finished the night with dessert and dancing. This all seemed like fairytale.

When we crawled into bed, Kendrick made love to me in a way he had never done before. The way he touched me, kissed me, licked me, and even stroked me was so passionate. He paid attention to the way my body reacted to everything

In The Name of Love

he was doing until I was fully satisfied.

Once he was off to sleep, I laid in bed looking at the ring. All I could do was wonder. Was this a fresh start? With all we've been through, was it enough, was this really him changing?

BREANNA J.

Chapter Eight

A few weeks had passed by and life seemed great. All the worries and drama that I was dealing with had seemed to fade away. Keyz was shockingly doing everything that he promised he was going to do when we got engaged. We haven't been fighting or arguing and every day. It seemed like he was sending me more wedding stuff than I was sending him. I could honestly say I was the happiest I had been in a while.

Things was even going good for little miss Kim. She was such a great kid. Kendrick and I offered her a room at our house, but she declined. She wanted to stay on her own and be an adult. I couldn't knock her. So, instead, I made a deal with her that if she went back to school and finished her senior year, she could stay in one of our empty apartments. She agreed with no hesitation.

She went back to school immediately. She had work to catch up on, but she did it like a champ. The girl was pretty and smart, which reminded me so much more of me. She would come to the shop and show me her work. She was acing the stuff with flying colors after being out of school for months. She didn't even let being in a new school bother her. It made me feel almost like a proud parent to see her doing so good and smiling. She looked so much better now than when I first met her. Her skin was glowing. She was putting on weight in all the right places. She was smiling more.

The vibe me and her had was priceless. I did everything I could to keep her out the streets. I helped rebuild her wardrobe. I got her furniture for her apartment and even gave

In The Name of Love

her a job at the shop after school as a braider so she could have money in her pockets. Her returning to the strip club was damn sure not about to happen under my watch. To make sure of that, I sent Keyz up to the strip club one day to talk to the owner, Monty. I wanted to make sure that Kim left that club clear and free.

I learned in that business that a lot of times these club owners treated these girls like they were pimping them, and no matter how much they tried to get out, they couldn't. Keyz never really told me what happened at the meeting. He just told me it was handled. As a reward for handling it and making sure Kim was good, I handled him in a special way that night.

A few days later, Kim got some flowers at the salon with a card that read that it was a pleasure to have her around and to not worry about anything. He wished her the best. It was signed by Monty. We were both happy. She told me it was like she was getting a second chance at life and she owed it all to me.

I told her it wasn't me. I told her that it was God, only he could have put us in the same area that day to become attached to each other the way we were now.

In my mind, she brought me just as much happiness as I brought her. I loved having her around. She was like the little sister I never had. When we reopened the shop, she was right there with me and I was glad because business was jumping like nothing ever happened. I was sure after old girl had destroyed the shop with clients there, my business was going to suffer, but to my surprise, all our clients returned and

BREANNA J.

laughed it off.

Business was going so good that we had the shop open almost 7 days a week.

Today was one of the days that all of us where there and working. Conversation was jumping and we were getting clients in and out. It was a cool vibe until Katrina's client got to talking and got everyone's attention. She was telling us how her younger sister had got herself mixed up in a love triangle a few weeks ago.

She said that the dude she was messing with was some big shot drug dealer in the city and they had been kicking it for a few years. The guy treated her so well. He was paying her rent and buying her stuff. He was telling her that he cared about her and anything else she needed to hear, which made her leave the dude she was originally with when she met him. She then told us that not too long ago the dude's wife caught them in a hotel room and ended up hitting her sister in the head with the butt of a gun. The girl had said that the wife had busted her sister's head open and the nigga didn't even make sure she was good. He chased after his wife and left her in the hotel by herself to find a way to the hospital to get stiches

Katrina, Tasha, Kim and I looked at each other but kept working.

The girl went on to say that her sister pulled up on the girl at her job the next day to get a one on one with the girl, but the girl wouldn't face her. She said instead the dude showed up and told her to leave and that he was done with her. He told her that he loved his wife and that if she mentioned his

IN THE NAME OF LOVE

name, his wife's name or this situation at all, he would be the person to take her life.

I smiled, and in my head, I was cheering.

Yes bitch, I win, you lose, he's mine, I'm the wife, I got the ring.

Though these were the thoughts in my head nothing was said out loud. Not because I was scared but because I was in business mode right now and Katrina, Tasha and Kim didn't know I was engaged. Every day before I got to the shop I took off my ring and put it in my purse. When I was on my way home, I would put it back on. I wasn't ready for the girls' judgement or reaction to me marrying Keyz because they didn't like the hurt he was causing me.

The girl kept talking about how she was going to find out who the guy and the wife was because she owed her sister a head up fight she had to get three stitches in her forehead.

I tuned the girl out until she said how her sister told her to leave the situation alone because she recently had hit the guy up about two weeks ago and told him she was pregnant.

I dropped the flat iron that was in my hands.

I was frozen, stuck, and in disbelief of what I just heard. This couldn't be true. Keyz couldn't be having a baby with no side line hoe that I had given the business to. I mean the bitch didn't even look better than me.

I picked up the flat iron and asked my client to excuse

BREANNA J.

me for a moment.

I went to my office and closed the door. I wanted to scream from the top of my lungs, but I couldn't. Just when things were looking good and these hoes were out of my life, here we go again.

I paced back and forth in my office.

Kim came in behind me.

As soon as our eyes met, I burst into tears.

I spoke while crying, "Really, Kim? Really? More bullshit for me to deal with. The nigga asked me to marry him just so I can find out he got a baby on the way by a side bitch. Is that what he is doing with the extra money he is making that he thinks I don't know about? Spending it on this bitch and their soon to be kid.'

Kim tried to calm me.

"Sasha, don't cry, relax. You know I'm always down to run down on a hoe. We can make sure that there is no baby for him to take care of. And, when the fuck did Keyz ask you to marry him and why am I just now finding out?"

I was so worked up and talking fast that I didn't realize that I had told my own secret.

"Kim, it's not just the baby, though; it's the fact that he asked me a few weeks ago to marry him. He did this grand old proposal, but there is always a secret coming out the clos-

IN THE NAME OF LOVE

et. Please don't tell Katrina or Tasha about the engagement. I've been taking off my ring every day before coming in here because I am just not ready to hear anyone's opinion on my life."

"Man, who cares what others have to think. If Sasha is happy and wants to marry Keyz, there is nothing that Katrina, Tasha or even I can say that matters. This is your life, Sasha. Fuck what people got to say. People are going to have their opinions, no matter if it's good, bad or to please them. And honestly, we don't even know if that bitch is telling the truth out there. Her and her sister could be liars. You know this is the beauty shop. Bitches come here to gossip because they know it's going to get back to whoever they are talking about. She clearly said her sister didn't tell her who it was, so maybe she is thinking that by telling all this info, the person will come to her. Either way, fix your face and come back out here and get this money. Don't let no hoe see you sweat, and tonight when you get home, you check that nigga."

"Thanks boo, I needed that talk."

Kim was younger than me but at that moment she had given me the talk I needed. It was a grown woman to woman talk.

We hugged and Kim went back out to the salon floor.

I got myself together and followed behind her with a smile on my face like nothing ever happened. Deep down inside, my mind and heart was racing.

I refused to keep being in the dark about things. I refused

BREANNA J.

for my shop to keep being the place where these bitches decided to be bold and tell what was going on in my life. This man had me all the way fucked up. Everything he had was in my name. I couldn't understand why he wanted to keep playing with me. The cars, the house, phone, bank accounts, rental property, it was all legally mine. I controlled the show. I was the boss and it was time I started to act like it.

In The Name of Love

Chapter Nine

We all finished up for the day around the same time. We straightened straighten up our stations and closed the shop. Kim and I went out to my car.

As I drove, I could see Kim looking at me out of the corner of my eye.

I blurted out, "What, Kim? What you want to say?"

Kim answered, "Nothing... No, I'm lying. Sasha, so what the fuck are we going to do about this shit going on with Keyz and that girl?"

I started to laugh because it seemed like Kim was madder than I was.

Kim looked at me, all confused.

She asked, "What did I miss? I'm serious. What are we going to do? This nigga Keyz not going to keep playing you. He needs to know that you know about his baby that's on the way. And that bitch need to know she'll never be you and that you're not going nowhere."

"Kim, don't worry about it. I'm a handle it. I'll be damned if I keep being taken advantage of. Believe me, both of them will feel my anger."

BREANNA J.

Kim smiled.

I pulled up to her apartment and dropped her off. Once she got out the car and went into the house, I sat outside for a while. I had to think of what the hell I was going to do.

While I sat there, my phone rang.

"Hello," I answered.

"Sasha?"

The voice coming through my car speakers sounded so familiar, but I couldn't put a face or name with the voice.

"Yes? May I ask whose calling?" I said back to the voice.

"This is Tony," the voice responded.

"How can I help you, Officer Tony?" I asked.

"Hey Sasha, I was wondering if you would have any free time where me and you can meet? Maybe over coffee or dinner. You know, just something casual."

I looked around, confused.

Tony must have called the wrong line because why the hell would I dare need to meet with him.

"What would we be meeting about and can my fiancé join this meeting?" I asked Tony in a sassy way.

IN THE NAME OF LOVE

You could tell from the long moment of silence that Tony didn't know that Keyz and I had gotten engaged.

"You and Keyz are engaged?" he asked.

"Yes, we are," I said proudly.

"Ummm well.... this meeting would go best if it was just us two," he said.

This nigga must have been stupid. First, he popped up at the shop a few weeks ago and didn't want me to tell Keyz, and now he wanted to meet without Keyz. This dude had me all the way fucked up, but shit, I'd play along and see what the hell this meeting was about.

I told Tony I would let him know when my schedule was free and hung up.

I figured I had sat in front of Kim's house long enough, so I pulled off and drove home. The whole way home I was in deep thought between what this meeting with Tony was about and how to get Keyz to tell me if he had a baby on the way. Then, the light bulb went off and I picked up my phone

Ring! Ring! Ring!

Katrina answered, "Hey Sash', what's up?"

"Nothing, I need a favor."

As I knew, Katrina was down.

Breanna J.

"Sure, anything."

"It's about that chick that was in your chair today doing all that talk about me and Keyz's situation," I told her.

"Her name is Trisha. What about her?"

"Find out what her sister's name is and where she works. Find out where she be and who she be with. I want to know it all."

"I got you."

I expressed my thanks.

"Thanks, and remember no paper trail. It shouldn't be able to point back to us that we did research about her."

"I got you."

"Thanks," I said again.

We hung up as I pulled up to the house. I could tell that Kendrick wasn't home yet, so I went in the house and set up my idea. I made dinner and set up the bedroom with rose petals, candles, and hot oil.

I filled the bathtub with extremely hot water, bubbles and rose petals, so that way, by time he came home, it would be nice and cool.

I put a bottle of wine and two wine glasses on the sink counter. Then, I played Trey Songz through the Bluetooth

In The Name of Love

speakers.

When Keyz got home, I made it my business to be in the bathtub. I could hear him walking through the house downstairs. He must have followed the sound of the music and the smell of the candles because before I knew it, he was standing in the bathroom door way looking at me.

I told him to get undressed and join me.

With no hesitation, he stripped down and hopped right in with me.

I let him sit in the front and lay on me in the tub while I rubbed on his chest and finished my glass of wine. I wanted him to feel like tonight was all about him because it was. I was going to seduce him and get him drunk and let his drunk ass tell me everything I wanted to know.

I poured him a glass a wine and handed it to him.

He threw it back in one swallow.

"Long day, bae?" I asked him.

"Yeah, but nothing I can't handle. You know ya man got this."

I smiled and said, "Yeah, my man got this" as I poured him another glass. "What exactly is going on? Maybe I can help. You know behind ever strong man is a strong woman keeping him uplifted," I said to him.

BREANNA J.

"Nothing major bae, little stupid shit. Did you start picking out a wedding dress yet?" he asked.

The question had thrown me off because I hadn't thought about a wedding dress not even once. Honestly, with my mom being gone and my brother not being here, it was hard to even picture a wedding. Who was going to cry when I finally stepped out in the prefect dress after trying on fifty of them? Who was going to smile ear to ear while walking me down the aisle because they were so proud? Who was going to fill my side of the church that my family and friends were supposed to be on?

"No, I didn't pick one out yet," I told him.

"While why don't you, Kim, Katrina and that Tasha girl go and try some out?" he suggested.

"Maybe, I'll see what they say," I said while rubbing his head looking off.

"Bae, I want this wedding to be everything you ever dreamed of. There is nothing that you can't have. If you want it, you got it. There is no limit as far as budget."

I smiled and held back the tears I had in my eyes. It was shit like this when I was mad at him that could make me change my mind. He could be such an asshole at one moment and such a lover at the other.

I eventually got out the tub before I started to wrinkle, but I wanted to keep my plan in motion so I turned on the hot water to make the water a little warmer for Keyz. Then, I sat

IN THE NAME OF LOVE

on the edge of our tube and I washed him.

Once he seemed to be relaxed, I started up another conversation with him. I pretended to listen and care.

When he asked me about my day, I told him, "Same old same old; the salon was packed, but we made it through. There was a bunch of chatty bitches in there running their mouth. Like always, about this and that, who's having a baby by who and who's a dead beat."

He laughed and made a comment that women did talk and gossip a lot.

I just looked at him. This man had no idea that his dirt had made it back to my business for the second time. After a while, I asked whether he was ready to get out and go eat.

He made a comment about being ready to eat me, but I acted like I didn't hear him.

He got out the tub and I oiled him down and massaged him. He returned the favor because he couldn't seem to keep his hands off of me.

Once I was able to get out of his grasp, I told him to relax in bed and gave him the TV remote.

I went downstairs and prepared his plates and poured him a glass of Henny. I came back upstairs.

I entered the room and Keyz had a big stupid looking smile on his face.

BREANNA J.

"Damn bae, a nigga could get use to this; I got a bubble bath with you, massage, and dinner served to me in bed. What did I do to deserve all this?" he asked.

I smiled and said, "Anything for you, Daddy" as I watched Keyz eat.

As he got close to finishing his food, I asked him, "Bae, can I ask you something?"

He smiled and said, "Yes beautiful, anything. Wassup?"

"How do you feel about a baby?" I asked him as I damn near stared a hole into the side of Keyz's head.

Keyz damn near choked on the food he had in his mouth.

"Sasha, do you want to have a baby?" he asked, kind of confused.

"Yes, of course, I do. I mean, I am your wife, well soon to be wife, so why not grow our family? Neither one of us has kids." I paused and looked at Keyz. "Unless you have a reason why you don't want to," I said to him.

Keyz put his plate on the nightstand and gave me a kiss.

"Bae, I've been waiting for you to be ready to have my baby," he said with a smile.

I kissed him back and gave him a seductive look.

"I'm ready," I said as I laid back in the bed.

In The Name of Love

As Keyz climbed on top of me, he looked me in my eyes and said, "I love you."

BREANNA J.

Chapter Ten

Keyz and I made passionate love until he fell asleep.

Once he was asleep, I laid there thinking to myself, *Damn, that plan didn't go as planned.*

Since I couldn't sleep, I figured I'd clean up and pick up Keyz's clothes and other mess. As I carried his clothes over to the dirty clothes basket, his pocket started to vibrate. I took the phones out his pocket and looked at them.

One phone was a prepaid phone that he talked drug business on. The other was the phone that he had on my phone plan.

I started to walk towards the nightstand to put them on the charger when Keyz's iPhone started to vibrate again. My heart was telling me just put it next to him on the nightstand, but my mind was telling me to look for answers.

I looked over at Keyz in bed. He was sound asleep. I clicked on the iPhone screen and tried to unlock it. The first code I put in failed.

"Damn," I said out loud.

I looked over at Keyz and he was still asleep. I looked at his finger.

"… Hell, nah I'll get caught…" I whispered.

IN THE NAME OF LOVE

I stood there thinking. Then it came to me. I tried 0803. It worked. It popped in my mind because it was Keyz's pin number for his debit cards and he played it when he played the lottery. It was also his mom's birthday and meant so much to him now that she was gone.

I took the phone and went downstairs to the den. I stared at the phone for a while questioning myself.

Sasha, are you really going to do this? Are you going to set yourself up to find something just because you're looking for it?

I picked up the phone and started going through his call logs. Then, I realized how dumb that was. This nigga was a drug dealer. He didn't save numbers. Most of the people he talked to used prepaid phones or called his prepaid phone.

I checked the text messages and they were clean. Nothing at all for me to find. My heart was relieved but in also a little in disbelief. Either he was a deleting his texts or he really had turned over a new leaf.

I sat the phone down on the desk in the den.

"Damn Sasha, you went through this man's phone for no reason," I said to myself.

Then, the phone buzzed.

I looked down and it was a Facebook message.

"What the fuck? Since when does this nigga have Face-

BREANNA J.

book?" I asked as I clicked on the message.

When I opened it, it was a conversation between Keyz and a Simone Cruz.

Simone: *So how can I prove to you that I am pregnant with your baby?*

What the fuck? I thought to myself.

I scrolled to the top of the message and read everything that popped up.

Simone: *Well, since you call yourself being done with me and you've blocked me from calling and texting you, I thought I'd tell your ass that I'm pregnant. You are going to be a part of this baby's life, Keyz, so you better get your girl under control and face me or I'ma tell the other secret that we have.*

I immediately clicked on the girl's profile picture.

It's her, I thought to myself.

All the shit I heard today at the shop had to be true because here she was in this man's Facebook inbox. My heart was racing and my blood was boiling as I clicked back to the message.

I took a moment to calm down before reading the rest of the messages because Lord knows I was ready to go upstairs and flip out on this man.

I took a deep breath and finished reading.

In The Name of Love

Keyz: *Simone, leave me the fuck alone with your crazy ass. I ain't get your dumb ass pregnant. If you are pregnant, it's not mine. When I did fuck you, I made it my business to put a condom on and flush the condom when we were done. Your ass just hurt because you can't get this dick no more or any money. You're trying to make my girl mad and hurt her so that she will leave me. But even still, I wouldn't dare be with your ass. You're a hoe.*

I read the message and in my head I was screaming, *Yes bae, tell her. Talk that shit. I mean, you wouldn't have to deal with the shit if you never fucked the bitch, but at the end of the day, you're correcting it.*

After that, I could see that Simone had called Keyz through Facebook Messenger, but he didn't answer. Then, it went to a message of Simone saying that Keyz wasn't shit and that he was a fuck nigga. I was even concerned with that part. Now that I had the info I needed, I could make my move.

I headed back upstairs. I didn't want Keyz to know that I went through his phone, so I had to do something. I dropped the phone in the dirty clothes basket with the clothes that Keyz had took off that night. I was surprised that all this time Keyz stayed asleep.

I made sure everything was cleaned up and all candle were out before snuggling up in bed next to Keyz. I laid there and just looking at him. This man had the power to make me completely crazy but still love him. It was a feeling that I couldn't understand some days or even explain.

As I got comfortable in bed, Keyz moved around to get

BREANNA J.

comfortable as well.

He opened his eyes and looked at me.

"What you are still doing up, bae," he asked.

"Nothing. I just cleaned up and made sure the candles were out," I answered with a smile.

"Come here," he said as he moved the covers for me to get on top of him.

I laid on top of him with my head on his chest, listening to his heart beat. He wrapped his arms around me tightly and I relaxed and let my body rest.

IN THE NAME OF LOVE

Chapter Eleven

The next morning, Keyz woke me up looking for his phones. I told him I didn't see them and asked him where was the last place he had it. He said that they were in his pants pockets. I innocently told him that I picked up the pants he had on last night and put them in the dirty clothes basket so the room wouldn't smell.

He rushed over to the basket and pulled everything out like a mad man. When he found them, he checked them both.

I sat up in bed.

"Is everything okay?" I asked him.

I was looking to see if he had any idea that I had been in his phone.

"Yes bae, it's all good. I found them," he said as he walked back towards the bed.

"What you got planned for today?" I asked him.

He sat on the edge of the bed while still looking at his phones and said, "I got a few moves to make with Pookie and then I'm coming home to you," e said.

I smiled.

"Okay well, I'm go to Kim house for a few. So we can go over some things for the shop."

BREANNA J.

As Keyz sat on the edge of the bed, I tried to see over his shoulder to see what he was doing in his phone, but when I finally got in a position where I could see the screen, he hit the lock button and stood up.

"Okay bae, I'm out. Give me a kiss," he said.

We kissed and Keyz went downstairs. Moments later, I heard my door close and his car start.

Once I knew he was out the driveway, I jumped up and got ready. I got fully dressed. I grabbed my purse and headed downstairs.

I walked in the kitchen to get a bottle of water before I left and there was a note on the table and a thousand dollars.

"Just because I love you. Love, Keyz."

I grabbed the money and a bottle of water and stuffed them both into my purse. I headed out.

I rushed over to Kim's house. She came to the door still looking half sleep with boy shorts and a tank top on with her nipples hard as a rock.

"Sasha, what you doing here this early?" she asked as she stretched.

"Girl, it's not early; it's almost noon. Why do you look like you just rolled out of bed?" I asked, pushing my way through the door.

IN THE NAME OF LOVE

"Girl, go get your laptop," I told her.

Kim went back to her room and got her laptop. She had thrown on some sweatpants and came back to the living room.

She sat down on the couch next to me.

"We ordering supplies for the shop?" she asked.

"Nah, I got someone I want you to look up," I said as I gave her a look to let her know that this was serious.

"Oh shit, who we are looking up?" she asked.

Kim flipped the laptop open and girl on girl porn popped up on the screen.

"Damn Kim," I said as I laughed.

She laughed too and said, "My bad. Don't judge me! I am in here lonely and horny. But any who, who's the person we are looking up?" she asked as she closed the webpage.

"I want you to look up a Simone Cruz on Facebook," I said.

Kim's face looked a little confused.

"Why are you looking like that?" I asked her.

"That name sounds so damn familiar," she said as she logged into Facebook.

BREANNA J.

She put the name in the search and Simone popped up.

"Her?" Kim asked.

"Yes, her," I said.

"I know her," Kim said.

"How?" I asked curiously.

"We went to school together. She's only like 20. She just graduated like a year or two ago. She had been trying to talk to me since I could remember."

I looked at Kim. I remembered she told us in general conversation one day at the shop that she was into girls but never would I have imagined that the same chick that was fucking my soon to be husband was also trying to fuck my newfound sister.

Kim looked at me.

"Wassup Sasha, why are we looking her up?"

I looked at Kim.

She screamed, "What?"

I looked at her and said, "That's the bitch I caught in the hotel room with Keyz."

Kim's eyes got big.

In The Name of Love

"So, what are we going to do?" Kim asked.

I sat and thought for a while in silence. I wanted to know all the information I could about this girl and whether she was pregnant by my man or not. I also wanted to know how long this situation had been going on.

I looked Kim in the eyes and said, "Make that bitch fall in love with you."

Kim smirked.

"When it's all said and done, this bitch will know the hurt she helped him make me feel," I told Kim.

Kim put her head down and went to typing away. She was laughing as she typed. I knew no matter what, Kim had my back and was down to ride for me.

As I sat waiting for Kim to do her job, my phone started to ring. I looked down at my phone and seen the unknown number.

I sighed.

"This better not be someone playing on my phone," I answered the phone. "Hello."

"Hello, may I speak to Sasha Brown?" the voice said.

"This is she," I said still trying to understand who was on my phone.

BREANNA J.

"I am sorry to be a bother, but my name is Officer Nicholas Murry. I am reaching out to see if there is a good time I can schedule to meet with you about a case I have here in the office," the voice said.

"What case? I am a busy woman and I don't have time for the games at all," I said back to him

With how I grew up, cops were not our friends and if they wanted you to come in, they wanted you to snitch. I wasn't going out like that.

"I would like to talk to you about the death of you brother, Calvin," the cop said.

My heart dropped as I let the phone go. It was like I was reliving the night all over again. The night I stood in my own living room and got the call from the police that my brother had been gunned down in his car in a parking lot.

"Hello? Sasha? Hello?" he said into the phone.

I kneeled and picked up the phone.

"Officer Murry, how dare you call my phone speaking of my fuckin' brother that has been dead for over two years now! When he died, you fuckin' cops worked on his case for a few weeks before labeling it as a cold case. Now, you want to have a meeting about his death? Fuck you!" I said and then hung up.

I was so stuck in the conversation that I didn't notice that Kim was standing right next to me, looking confused.

IN THE NAME OF LOVE

"Sasha, who was that? Are you okay?" she asked.

By this time, I was shaking and I fell to the ground.

Kim sat on the floor next to me.

The tears poured down my eyes.

"That was a cop wanting to talk about CJ," I told Kim.

"CJ is dead," Kim said with a confused face.

"Exactly, it's been two fuckin' years. I refuse to reopen this hurt or to relive this all over again!" I cried.

Kim wrapped her arms around me.

I screamed, "Why is this my life?"

Kim and I sat on the floor. I cried and she comforted me.

After a few minutes, a ding came from Kim's laptop. Then, the laptop dinged a few more times.

Kim got up and looked at the computer.

"She wrote me back," Kim said.

Kim: *What's up hun? How you been? Long time no hear.*

Simone: *What's up gorgeous? I was just thinking about your fine ass. I'm good, just pregnant; how are you?*

Breanna J.

"Sasha look," she said to me.

I came and read the messages over Kim's shoulder. My heart started to race.

"So, what you want me to do?" Kim looked at me, eyes wide as if she was a child looking for guidance.

With the most evil voice I could muster up, I looked at Kim and told her, "Pull that bitch in, get her by any means necessary."

Kim gave me this evil smirk that kind of scared me.

Kim: *Word? How far along are you?*

Simone: *3 months*

Kim: *Word? Congratulations to you and your dude.*

Simone: *No dude. I'm single with a deadbeat ass baby daddy already*

Kim: *Damn, that's crazy because I know your fine as hell still, pregnant and all.*

Simone: *Shit, don't make me blush! You know I been at you and wanting you for a while, but you wanted the hot boys with money.*

Kim: *Shit, I was trying to survive. But now I am stable. Not to mention you were chasing the dope boys and trying to have me at the same time.*

IN THE NAME OF LOVE

Simone: *Well, shit ya ass was fine and them niggas wasn't doing nothing for you that I couldn't do better.*

Kim: *oh word?*

Simone: *Yeah, shit! Pregnant and all, I can still do you better than them*

Kim: *oh, talk that shit shorty*

Simone: *Fuck talking let me show you.*

Kim turned around and looked at me with that same evil smirk.

"Got her."

We both laughed.

This bitch didn't even know what was in store for her.

"Offer to take the hoe to dinner," I told Kim.

Kim looked and me and with a roll of the neck told me, "Sasha, I love you, but I'm not trickin' on this hoe."

I laughed.

"I'll pay for it," I said.

Kim turned back to the laptop and started typing again.

Kim: *Well let's go to dinner. We can talk and get caught up.*

BREANNA J.

Simone: *Fine. My treat*

Kim: *Okay bet*

Simone: *okay text my phone (614)500-2922*

Kim turned to me, "So, what now?"

I spoke, "First, give me that number. I want to see if that's the number that calls or texts Keyz's phone. After that, it's simple. You're going to play that bitch while getting me all the info I want."

I grabbed my purse and got ready to leave Kim's house.

Before I could make it to the door, my phone started to ring again. My heart skipped a beat. If it was that officer calling back again, I promised I would lose my shit and never answer my phone again.

I looked down and saw that it was Keyz. I put on my excited voice so he wouldn't know I was up to no good.

"Hey baby," I said as I answered the phone.

"Wassup beautiful, what are you doing?" Keyz asked.

"Just getting ready to leave Kim's house," I told him.

"Cool, meet me somewhere?" Keyz asked.

"Where?' I asked.

IN THE NAME OF LOVE

"I'll text you the address. Keep your phone close by."

We both said our goodbyes and hung up.

"Kim, I'm out," I told her as I walked towards the door.

"Iight, I'll see you at the shop tomorrow after school," Kim said as she walked me to the door.

I walked out the house and down to my car. By the time I got in the car, Keyz's text came through with the location. The address seemed familiar, but it didn't ring a bell.

BREANNA J.

Chapter Twelve

I pulled up to the address Keyz gave me and I couldn't believe I didn't remember that address. It was to the restaurant we had our first date at.

A gentlemen came to my car and helped me out. As he pulled off to go park my car I walked towards the door. I was trying to understand what was going on. The first time we had our date here, the place was packed. There was people coming in and out, but tonight there was none of that.

A garment bag with my name on it and a message that read, *change into me* laid across the hostess' desk. I grabbed the bag and went to the bathroom. Inside the garment bag was a beautiful all black gown with a heart shaped top and a very high split that almost looked like the one I had worn on our first date. At the bottom of the garment bag was a box. I opened it and inside was a pair of black open toe red bottoms, a gorgeous pair of earrings and a bracelet.

I changed into everything and came back out. This time, Keyz was standing at hostess' desk with a dozen of red roses. I walked up and kissed him.

"Hello beautiful," he said to me.

"Hello handsome," I said with a smile.

I looked around and started to notice there were no guest and very little staff.

IN THE NAME OF LOVE

"Keyz, where's everyone?" I asked him.

"Tonight is just me and you. You treated me so good last night that I wanted to return the favor," he said.

I looked around, confused.

"How did you pull this off, Keyz?" I asked, "And don't tell me you emptied one of our accounts to flex," I snapped at him a little with my hands on my hips.

Keyz laughed, "Baby no, I know the new owner and he owed me a favor."

I was no dummy. I knew that meant that Keyz sold the owner drugs and he hadn't paid up.

I gave Keyz a side eye and said, "Umm, okay."

Keyz walked me over to the table. He pulled out my chair and I sat down and he sat across from me.

The waiter came over and poured us both a glass of wine. Keyz gazed at me from across the table, smiling.

It actually made me blush.

"How was your day?" he asked.

"My day was fine. I spent most of it at Kim's house. How was yours?"

He said, "It was fine, the same old same old. Anything

BREANNA J.

new going on? I feel like we never get to really talk because we both are on the go."

I sat there and thought so many things screaming out in my mind that I wanted to say such as, "Yeah, I found out that you are making more money than you're telling me. I also found out about your soon to be baby momma Simone and oh yeah, your cop friend has been to the shop and calling my phone."

But instead, I kept my cool and said, "Not much outside of the fact that I got a disturbing call from the cops about CJ."

Keyz looked confused but shocked at the same time.

"What the fuck? What are they calling about now? He's been gone for two years and when we were looking for answers, they were no help," Keyz said.

"Exactly, but even getting the call was like reliving his death all over again. My heart dropped when the cop said his name," I told him, trying not to have a meltdown like I did at Kim's house.

"Baby, fuck the cops. We put CJ to rest in an honorable and respectful way. I'm not going to let them stress you out, especially not while we're trying to have a baby," Keyz said with a smirk.

I smiled at him. I honestly felt like Keyz was all I had. He was a dream come true and in some ways, my worst nightmare.

IN THE NAME OF LOVE

We sat and talked for longer. We ordered food and continued to talk.

Keyz kept gazing across the table at me.

"What Keyz, why do you keep looking at me like that?" I asked him, smiling.

"Nothing, just thinking how lucky I am. You are so beautiful and the empire that we have built together so far is unbreakable. When I first laid eyes on you, I knew I wanted you and everything you came with. I just didn't know how much I would be winning by having you."

I smiled and stood up. I leaned over the table and gave him a kiss.

After we ate, Keyz handed me an envelope.

"What's this?" I asked him.

"Open it," he told me.

I opened it and there was for two tickets to Jamaica inside. I held the tickets in my hands and looked at him.

"Jamaica?" I asked.

Keyz said, "Baby, a destination wedding of your dream. I felt like you were kind of detached from the whole wedding planning idea because neither of us have family here. So, I figured why not have a wedding in Jamaica? I have everything already arranged. All you have to do is sign the mar-

BREANNA J.

riage license, mail it and get on the plane."

My eyes started to water. It had been only a few weeks ago that this man asked me to marry him, and just that quick, he had planned basically our whole wedding.

"What about my dress?" I asked.

"Baby, you can have whatever dress you want. Hell, you can just wear your draws if you want, as long as you don't leave me hanging at the altar," Keyz answered.

I walked around the table and sat on Keyz's lap.

I gave him the best kiss and told him, "I'll be there."

As I sat on his lap, I said, "But.... I have one request."

Keyz just looked at me.

"I want Kim and the girls there."

Keyz nodded his head.

"Anything you want, my Queen."

I smiled.

The waiter came back and asked if we wanted dessert.

I told him yes, but it wasn't anything he had in the kitchen.

IN THE NAME OF LOVE

I looked at Keyz and mouthed, *Let's go.*

Keyz stood and pulled my chair out. He told me to head to his car.

I walked out and Keyz's car was right out front. I got in on the passenger side. As I waited, I slipped off the thong I had on.

Keyz came out to the car and got in.

"Phil, the owner, will have one of his guys bring your car to the house," he said.

I nodded.

"Do you want to go to a movie or a walk in the park?" he asked.

I took Keyz's hand and put it through my split to feel under my dress.

Then I looked him in the eyes and asked, "What do you think I want to do?"

Keyz smiled and said out loud, "Oh yeah? We are doing 90 all the way home," he said as he sped off.

BREANNA J.

Chapter Thirteen

The next day I woke to the man of my dreams and the murder in my worst nightmare.

As we laid in bed, I looked at him. He rested so peacefully.

My phone rung. I rolled over to answer it quickly before it woke Keyz.

"Hello," I answered.

It was Katrina.

"Hey Sash', what time you are coming in today?"

"I should be there within the next few hours. Why, what's up hun?"

"I want to tell you about some info I found out that you told me to get."

I answered, "Oh iight, I'll be there soon."

We hung up and I got up and got in the shower.

When I got out the shower, Keyz was sitting up on edge of the bed, facing the window on the phone. When he heard me open the bathroom door, he quickly rushed off the phone.

The last thing I heard him say was "Find out why" as he

In The Name of Love

hung up the phone.

I ignored it and grabbed my lotion. I sat on the edge of the bed on my side.

Keyz walked around the bed to my side and gave me a kiss on the cheek.

"Good morning, baby," he said.

"Good morning," I said.

Keyz walked over to our closet to find something to wear as he spoke to me.

"So, I'm going down to the travel agent today to see if I can get three more tickets for the girls to come. Will you be at the shop all day?"

I kept putting lotion on my body as I answered his question.

"Yes, I got a packed schedule today, I think."

Keyz grabbed some clothes out and laid them on the bed.

"Okay," he said.

I stood up and went to the closet.

As I walked past Keyz, he rubbed my stomach and said, "You are getting thick, girl!"

BREANNA J.

I looked at myself in the full-size mirror next to our closet. My stomach wasn't as flat as it was weeks ago but it was no big deal. I always picked up a little weight when Keyz stressed me out and then I would drop it.

I laughed and said, "Shut up, that's 'cause all you want to do is feed my ass lately like I'm a big girl or something. Shit, stop feeding me and buy me some gifts."

Keyz laughed and went into the bathroom.

I went in the closet and pulled out one of my pink sweatsuit and got dressed. Then, I grabbed my purse and some Jordans and went downstairs. I grabbed a water and a fruit bar. I also turned on the coffeepot for Keyz so that he could have his coffee before leaving the house.

I went to the door and reached in my purse for my keys.

Where the hell are my keys? I thought to myself.

Then I remembered that we left my car last night and the people were supposed to bring it back.

I went back upstairs.

Keyz had gotten out the shower by this time.

I walked in the room and he was back sitting on the edge of the bed with his phone in his hands.

"Bae," I said as I turned the corner into the room.

IN THE NAME OF LOVE

Keyz quickly put his phone down and he turned and looked at me.

"What's up bae, I thought you left?" he asked.

"I can't leave, my car isn't back!" I barked at him.

"Oh shit!" he said. "Take my car."

He handed me the keys off the nightstand.

I sighed as I took the keys out his hands. I hated driving his car because a few years ago when I was driving his car, a chick chased me down thinking I was him. That caused a big argument in our house because it was the first time that I had seen with my own two eyes that this nigga had other bitches out here besides me. After that, I tried to never drive his car unless I really had to.

I went outside and got in Keyz's car.

On my way to the shop, Kim texted me and asked me to pick her up from school. She said she wasn't feeling well. So, I bypassed the shop and went and got my shorty.

When I got to the school, Kim was already sitting outside waiting on me.

She hopped in and asked, "When did you get a new car?"

"This is Keyz's car, girl, and what's wrong with you? You want some ginger ale before you go in the house?" I asked her.

BREANNA J.

Kim leaned back into the passenger seat and told me to take her to the shop with me. I didn't know what was going on because she seemed sick. She wasn't her normal bubbly self, but she didn't want to go home.

We pulled up to the shop and I turned the car off.

"Kim, what's wrong?" I asked her.

Tears started to roll down Kim's face.

"Kim, what's wrong? Do I need to go up to the school?"

Kim leaned down and opened her book bag. She pulled out a piece of paper and handed to me.

When I looked at the paper, it was a picture of Kim and around it read, *Former Stripper looking for fun call her*.

I grabbed Kim and held her.

"Kim, I am so sorry. I thought by sending you to this school outside the hood you wouldn't have to face this," I told her.

Kim said, "At least if I kept my ass in the hood, I would be comfortable. At that school, they feel like I'm an outcast. No matter how smart I am, I will never fit in and now this. Now, I have to go back there to this mainly white school and deal with them treating me like a black hoe," she continued to cry.

"Kim, I promise I'll figure this out for you. I am so sorry,

In The Name of Love

baby," I told her as I tried to comfort her.

Kim looked me in my eyes.

"Sasha, can I just get my G.E.D and work here at the shop? I mean, I always have clients looking to come in and I'm always limited on the number of clients I can take because of school."

I was so hurt to hear Kim say that she would just rather get her G.E.D. She was so close and I knew the girl was so smart. But, I'd do anything to keep Kim happy because seeing her like this was not acceptable.

I smiled and looked at Kim.

"Would shopping make you feel better? Maybe once you feel better then you can think about everything once you're in a better mood."

Kim sat up and wiped her face.

"Nah, let's go in here and get this money because my mind is already made up."

We got out the car.

My heart was heavy, but if she wanted to go on with the day like nothing happened, I had to respect that.

As the day went on, I watched Kim in the shop. It amazed me that she was so young but had mastered how to hide that things were going wrong in her life. This young

Breanna J.

girl was just crying on my shoulder in the car. Right now, I watched as she stood before me interacting with her customers and everyone like nothing had happened, like the hurt was never there.

As I worked on my client, my phone rung, I asked my client to give me a moment while I stepped aside and picked up the phone. When I answered, it was Keyz.

"Hey baby," I spoke into the phone.

"Hey, so I got some good news."

"What's up?" I asked.

I got your three girls and Sean tickets on the same flight as us and hotel rooms in the same hotel as us. But here is the kicker, because the travel agent literally pulled strings to get this, I must have everyone's info to her by tomorrow at the latest."

I screamed with excitement, "Oh my God, are you serious? Okay okay, I'll call you back."

I quickly hung up on Keyz and went back to my station. I put my phone on my station.

"Ladies, Ladies," I said as I stepped in the middle of the shop floor so everyone could see me.

Everyone looked at me and I went on to ask, "How would you ladies feel about closing the shop for a whole week in about three weeks?"

IN THE NAME OF LOVE

All the girls looked confused.

Katrina asked, "Now why in the hell would we want to do something like that and mess up our money?"

I stood there looking at them all and Kim busted out and said, "Well, Sasha? Why would you ask us something like that?"

I smiled and said, "Because in three weeks I will become Mrs. Keyz and he has paid for all three of you to come with me to Jamaica to share my wedding day with me."

All the girls screamed and ran to hug me.

"When the hell did you get engaged?" Katrina asked as she hugged me.

"He asked me a month or two ago. I was just scared to tell y'all after we had that talk and y'all saying I should leave him," I said with my head down.

Tasha grabbed my face.

"No matter how we feel about Keyz, we will always be there to support you. If he makes you happy enough to marry, then so be it," I smiled.

"Kim I want you to be my maid of honor. Katrina, I want you to beat my face, and Tasha, I want you to slay a lacefront on me," I said to them while we hugged.

They all nodded and we all smiled as I began to cry.

BREANNA J.

Katrina pulled away from our group hug and asked, "Girl, what is wrong with your bi-polar self?"

I wiped my tears and admitted, "All this time, I thought I was alone and that my wedding wouldn't be special because my mom and brother are gone, but you guys have stepped in and filled this void that I thought I would have forever where my family was supposed to be. You guys are the best family I could ever ask for."

Kim looked at me and said, "Girl, we are rocking with you until the wheels fall off."

Candy butted in and said, "Shit, and once they fall off, I am still there with you pushing the car, this is a forever love, no matter what."

We all laughed.

Mrs. Townsend who was sitting in my chair cleared her throat.

She said, "Sasha baby, I am proud of you and your man, but I'm trying to get fine for my man right now."

We all busted out laughing again because Mrs. Townsend was almost seventy and got around fine and looked even better.

I went over and hugged her.

"I am so sorry Mrs. Townsend, let's get you looking right for Mr. Townsend."

In The Name of Love

"Its fine baby, just make my curls tight and right because Fred will help loosen them tonight." Mrs. Townsend said with some sass in her voice.

My mouth dropped.

Katrina, Kim, Tasha and I looked at each other with wide eyes.

Mrs. Townsend fixed herself in the chair and spoke again.

"Why y'all look shocked? You youngns aren't the only ones getting y'all groove on."

We all laughed.

It was moments like this that made being a salon owner so perfect.

As the day ended and the last client left, I told the girls to make sure that they give me their info so I could give it to Keyz. Tasha and Katrina gave me their information after they cleaned their station and then they left. Kim finished cleaning our stations while I went to the office to do the books.

When she was done, she came back and sat in the office with me.

I looked at Kim and asked, "Kim, if you drop out and get your G.E.D, what's your plan after that?"

Kim made a face as if she were thinking.

BREANNA J.

"I could get my C.N.A license and do hair here," she answered.

I frowned because that was not going to happen on my watch.

"Fuck no! You're not about to be like no average hood bitch," I told her.

Her having that idea was so disappointing to me. I loved this girl so much that I couldn't let her sell herself short, especially when I know she could achieve so much more.

"Let's do this, it's Wednesday. Skip school tomorrow and Friday. You can come here and work all day. Then come Monday, we can go in and speak to your guidance counselor.

Kim looked at me.

"Okay, but I'm going to Jamaica, no matter what. Fuck school!"

We laughed.

To me it was okay because at least she was open to possibly going back and seeing what else could happen.

In The Name of Love

Chapter Fourteen

After I did the books, Kim and left the shop.

In the car, Kim kept looking at her phone.

"You smiling pretty hard over there, who are you texting?"

Kim looked over at me and said, "Simone."

My interest sparked.

"So, what's happening with the date?" I asked her.

"It's Friday night. We are going to do dinner and a movie," she said.

Kim's phone went off again. She looked down and smiled again.

"Kim, you don't have go out with her. At the end of the day Keyz and I are three weeks away from getting married. Whatever he did before this don't matter. I am determined to be happily married and trusting my man," I said to Kim with a straight face.

"Sasha, are you sure because you know I will never betray you, not over this bitch. If you want to be happy with Keyz and leave this girl in the past, so be it, but can I at least get some head since I'm this far in? Because I can't lie, some of this stuff she's saying has my pussy jumping, Kim said to

BREANNA J.

me.

"T.M.I, Kim," I yelled and laughed at the same time.

As we pulled up to Kim's house, she said, "Look," and handed me the phone.

Simone: *Can I ask you a questions?*

Kim: *yeah whats up?*

Simone: *You wanna sit on my face?*

Kim: *Where did that come from? Your pregnant.*

Simone: *My stomach don't have nothing to do with my mouth*

Kim: *I mean I can't lie that question did just make my pussy wet. But....*

Simone: *I promise I'll make it way more wet. You'd never have another complaint about me or me being pregnant. Cause I'll keep you satisfied.*

Kim: *.....*

Simone: *So you going to let me?*

Kim: *when?*

Simone: *When you're ready?*

IN THE NAME OF LOVE

Kim: *It's been a while since I had anything sexual*

Simone: *that's perfect I want all of you... just be ready for me*

Kim: *tell me what you want to do to me?*

Simone: *whatever you let me*

Kim: *tell me what you want to do*

Simone: *I want to kiss your lips. I want to suck on your titties. I want to taste your skin. I want to suck on your clit I know it probably so pretty. I want you to ride my face. I really really want to fuck you with a strap.*

Kim: *Nah you can't fuck me with no strap but I can fuck you with one*

Simone: *How you gonna fuck me with one that's wasn't the plan.*

Kim: *Me getting fucked with one wasn't the plan either*

Simone: *I don't have to I just said I wanted to. Tell me what you want.*

Kim: *I want you to suck on my nipples and play with my clit. Active my super soaker.*

Simone: *and then?*

Kim: *I want you to kiss on my thighs and stomach, tease*

BREANNA J.

me a little bit.

Simone: *yes, I can definitely do that. Just don't fight me and don't run.*

Kim: *I doubt you make me run. Then when you do eat my pussy tell me how good it taste, suck on my clit. Rub on my nipples. But a finger in my ass. Then maybe I'll let you fuck me with a strap.*

Simone: *damn*

Kim: *What*

Simone: *I'll do everything you just asked and more.*

I can't lie. Their conversation had me a little turned on and I was all the way straight. I had to make sure that although getting her pussy sucked on sounded good, the family we had built together was more important.

"Kim, do you feel like you're up to do this? Like are you going to want to wife her after?" I asked her.

"Yes Sasha, why are you acting like this, is it 'cause you seen us talking about eating pussy? I am going to remain focus, no matter what. I know what the goal is," Kim answered me back with a snappy attitude.

"Kim I just don't want your feelings to get involved and you be stuck in the middle." I told her in a concerned voice.

Kim looked at me.

IN THE NAME OF LOVE

"Feelings? I lost those a while back. I am about to work this hoe how I used to work these niggas before you came into my life," Kim said with a genuine look in her eyes. As I pulled up to Kim apartment she turned and looked at me and said, "Sasha trust me, I got this."

She got the car.

I drove home.

When I arrived, the house was empty. There was no Keyz in sight. I went upstairs and sat at my vanity. There was so many thoughts going through my mind. Then, my phone rang. I took it out my purse and saw that it was Katrina calling.

"What's up, Katrina?" I answered.

"Hey boo; are you alone?"

"Yeah, why what's up?"

"So… remember when you asked me to do some digging and find out about that girl that came to the shop?" she asked.

"Yes; what did you find?"

"Well, you know my sister Courtney, right? Well, she got her medical assistant degree a few months back and now she's working at this OBGYN office and ummm…." Katrina hesitated.

"Umm, what?"

BREANNA J.

I waited for an answer.

"When I picked up Courtney today, I saw what I think was Keyz and that girl coming out of that office."

Oh, really. Hold on," I told her.

I put Katrina on hold and clicked over to the other line. I called Keyz.

He answered on the first ring.

"What's up, baby?"

"Nothing, just got home and you're not here. Where you at?" I questioned.

"I'm out in the hood making moves. Why? What's up? You need something?" he answered.

"I mean, I wanted my man to be home. I'm sure you been making moves all day."

"Sasha, if I don't work, we don't eat or pay for this wedding you want. I had to make all that money back that I gave to the travel agent to keep you happy."

"Yeah, whatever. I'm going to eat regardless of what you do. Remember, I still make my own money," I snapped.

"Sasha, what is wrong with you? What do you want from me? Because you're really at me."

In The Name of Love

"Nothing."

"I'm going to be home soon to give you all my attention and some of this loving. Are you going to cook or you want me to bring you home something to eat?" he had the nerve to ask.

"Nah, I'm good I'm about to step out with the girl tonight anyway."

"What? When the hell did you start going out during the week? Don't start acting crazy this close to the wedding. Just tell me what you want."

"Keyz, I don't want nothing anything but to go out and have a good time with my girls. Nothing crazy at all about that. We are going to go to a bar. Get some drinks and chicken."

"Yeah, okay."

Keyz hung up and I knew he was pissed.

I clicked back over to Katrina.

"Katrina?"

She answered, "Yes girl, what were you doing? I almost hung up."

"Get dressed. We're stepping out tonight. Invite Trisha and your sister, too. Say it's my bachelorette party."

BREANNA J.

"Umm, okay."

We hung up and I called Kim.

"Hey Sasha, what's up?"

"Get dressed. We are going out," I informed.

"Umm, okay," she agreed without question.

"I'll be there to get you."

I hung up with Kim and looked in the mirror. Somebody had me all the way fucked up and I was ready to get down to the bottom of it or at least remind this nigga what we had before he found himself in Jamaica alone. I was going to use every person that was brought up to get down to the bottom of everything. I had to do this before I put my name on any marriage papers or boarded any flight.

I went and took a shower and made sure to shave from top to bottom. When I got out the shower, I laid on the bed and for the first time in a long time, I took a nude and sent it to Keyz.

The message read: *stay awoke and wait for me.*

He texted back quick.

Damn, nah stay your ass home just like that. It'll be worth the wait.

I sent him back an *lol.*

In The Name of Love

I told him that I would see him when I get home, then I got up and got dressed. I did my hair, make-up and sprayed the perfume that always had Keyz all over me.

By the time I finished with that and found something to wear, Kim and Katrina were both texting me telling me they were ready.

I finished the final touches to my outfit and I headed towards the door. I stood at the door and looked at my phone. There had been no more texts from Keyz in the last two hours and he wasn't home yet.

I sent him a text that read *I'm leaving the house now*.

I waited a few minutes and there was no answer. I got in the car in my feelings. So, I turned on the Keyshia Cole station on Pandora.

I pulled off and headed to Kim's house. While driving, I kept looking at my phone expecting a text, call or something from Keyz, but there was nothing.

By the time I got to Kim's house, I was completely worried. My mind was racing. This man couldn't possibly be that mad. Maybe he was with the next woman or somewhere hurt.

Kim came out the house and got in the car screaming, "That's my shit" as Keyshia Cole's "Shoulda Let you Go" came through the car speakers.

I fixed my face and turned down the music.

BREANNA J.

"Let me call Katrina" I said.

I dialed Katrina's number and put the phone on speaker.

"Hello?"

"What's up? I got Kim, so where y'all want to go?"

"Cool, I got my sister, and Trisha said she'd met us there. I'm in a giving mood. Let's go see the strippers."

I looked at Kim and she nodded.

"I'm cool with that, I got my fake ID," Kim admitted.

"Okay, so what strip club?" I asked.

"Well, Pearl doesn't require us to have a man with us to get in," Katrina spoke.

"Okay, let's go there then."

"Alright, see y'all there shortly," Katrina said.

We hung up and headed to the club. As we drove, I filled Kim in on the information I had gotten from Katrina.

Kim sat and didn't say a word for a while.

"Well Sasha, she did have a doctor's appointment today. At least that's what she told me she was doing earlier when we were texting," Kim informed me.

In The Name of Love

"Mhmm, and did she say if the baby daddy was there with here?" I inquired.

"She doesn't talk about her baby daddy anytime we talk. And I thought you weren't pressing the issue no more? You said that you were giving Keyz a clean slate. Like, are you getting these ladies together to try to dig up some dirt?

"Drunk females tell all."

We laughed 'cause we knew it was true.

Kim and I arrived first and we sat in the car talking until the other ladies pulled up. Katrina pulled up next and parked on the side of us. A few moments later, Trisha pulled up and parked on the side of Katrina.

Katrina hopped out her Nissan Rogue and the rest of us followed. I was focused on the mission at hand, but I had to admit all these ladies had stepped out tonight looking on point. I was proud to be walking into the club with these four women. I was sure that were we doing our damn thing because the men were trying to holla and break their neck to look at us and the women were mean mugging.

I was dressed in an all-black skin tight jumpsuit that Keyz had told me to throw away after I tried it on for him. He said it showed the imprint of my pussy and he didn't even want niggas imagining how good the pussy he came home to was.

But shit, this jumpsuit had my ass and titties looking right and sitting right and my caramel knee-high boots with the

BREANNA J.

gold heel added to my look. I did my makeup real natural but made sure that my highlight was popping. Then, I pulled my hair back into a slick bun.

Kim had on a bodysuit with some fishnet stockings. It kind of looked like a leotard but she was pulling it off. She was giving a little side boob and a little side ass. It was just enough to see some of the flowers she had tattooed on her ass. Her burgundy thigh high boots put everything together.

Katrina's ass looked so crazy that I had to focus to see what she actually had on. Katrina had one of those asses that a nigga could sit his drink on and it wouldn't spill. That ass was resting safely in some black shorts with some red pumps. Katrina had on a black blazer on where she buttoned only the middle button so she showed a little belly. Her breasts were sitting nicely in a lace bra.

Courtney was the slimmest of us all but still a little thick. She had a short haircut and with her skin tone one would say she looked like Halle Berry. She had on a red leather Bodycon dress. It hugged her body perfectly, but her black pumps with the spikes on them made the outfit.

Trisha was dressed in black leather pants and a black corset. When she was at the shop, I had never noticed that she had a shape under the baggy scrubs I saw her in. Regardless, she was definitely something to look at; she had a cute face and nice body. She was rocking the 20 inch body weave bundles that we sold at the shop. Hell, if she wasn't my enemy's sister, I may have had kept her around to join me and Keyz for a threesome.

In The Name of Love

Katrina introduced everyone. We all smiled and hugged and then headed towards the door. It was like we should have been in a movie, in one of those scenes where they have the hot girls walking past guys in slow motion.

When we got to the door, the bouncers checked our IDs and patted us down. While no one was looking, I took my ring off and slide it into my purse. We entered the club and it was jumping. There was fine men and half naked ladies everywhere.

"Ladies, we're about to be lit! What do y'all want to drink? First round on me," Trisha said.

I ordered a double shot of Remy with a Red Bull. Kim and Courtney followed me and ordered the same thing. Trisha and Candy ordered Patron.

Once we all got our drinks, we went to find a booth to sit in near the stage.

Once everyone got comfortable, Kim started a conversation.

"Courtney, you're so pretty and you look so familiar. I never even knew Katrina had a sister. Why don't we ever see you come through the shop?"

Courtney answered back, "Me and Katrina have the same dad because our moms were bitter baby mamas. We didn't get to spend a lot of time together when we were kids, but when we got older, we made the decision to build a relationship. She does my hair but it's normally when the shop is closed

BREANNA J.

because of the hours I work."

I jumped in and asked, "Where do you work?" as if I didn't already know the answer to that.

"I work at the Sara Martin Health O.B.G.Y.N," Courtney answered.

Trisha butted in and said, "My sister goes there."

"Well, small world, what's your sister name? Is she a regular?" Courtney asked.

"Yeah, she should be a regular there seeing as though she is pregnant. You might have seen her and her baby father there today as matter a fact. Her name is Simone Cruz. I don't know her baby daddy's name. She won't tell us the deadbeat's name for some reason," Trisha told the table.

I butted in and asked, "Is this the same sister that you were telling us about at the shop?"

Trisha answered, "Yes, I guess her and the dude worked stuff out and now he's back around. My sister says that they have been messing around for years and even did some dirt together, so they can't let each other go. In her stupid ass mind, she thinks that they are Bonnie and Clyde. He's supposed to be sending her on a trip to Puerto Rico in three weeks to see our parents."

Candy looked at Trisha.

"Wow, I didn't know you were Puerto Rican, girl."

IN THE NAME OF LOVE

Trisha answered, "Yeah, my family's straight off the boat Rican. My dad brought my mom here while she was pregnant with our oldest sister. About three years ago, they decided they wanted to go back home; me and my 5 siblings haven't seen them since."

We all sat and listened to Trisha's story.

"But whatever, enough about me, my sister and that nigga I told her to leave alone. Let's get turnt the fuck up!" Trisha said.

One of the strippers came over and started dancing.

"This is what I like to see!" Trisha yelled.

"Me too!" Kim yelled, smiling and agreeing with Trisha as they both took money out of their purses and got close to the stripper.

I leaned over to Katrina.

"Trisha like girls?" I asked her.

She must have heard me because she turned around and said, "No need for the secrets. Yes, I like women. And oh yeah, the name is Trish, not Trisha. There is no need to be formal. This is not work. We are all here looking at ass together."

Then she looked at me and winked.

I got up and said, "Second round on me, y'all want the same thing?"

Breanna J.

Each girl said yes so I grabbed my purse and walked to the bar.

I heard Trisha behind me.

"Hold up Sasha, I'll come with you."

We walked over to the bar and waited for the bartender to come over to us.

"So Sasha… What's your story?" Trisha asked while looking me up and down.

I answered her, "Umm, my story is pretty simple. No family, business owner, independent, focused and soon to be married."

Trisha looked at me and nodded her head.

"Well, that's nice, but I'ma get to the point. I've come to the shop enough to have dreams about your fine ass. I know you got a man and all that, but I want you to come home with me tonight," Trisha said confidently. I began to speak, but Trisha cut me off.

"You don't have to answer right now, just know that I want you to let me taste you, that's all. No one ever has to know; just think about it and if you like it we can keep it just our secret. I will be your best kept secret," she said.

Before I could say anything, the bartender came over and asked what we were drinking. I turned my focus to her.

In The Name of Love

Chapter Fifteen

Once she had the drinks made, I reached out to hand her the money and another hand moved mine out the way.

"This round is on me ladies."

I looked to the right of me and there stood Tony.

I smiled.

"Hello, Ms. Sasha," he greeted me.

"Hello Tony."

Trisha tapped me on the shoulder.

"I'ma take these to the girls. Are you okay?" she asked.

"Yes I'm good, he's good people," I said as I looked at Tony.

This man was even finer then I remember. I didn't know whether it was the alcohol or the fact that Keyz was ignoring me, but I was ready to jump on this man right here in this club.

I looked him up and down.

"You are looking good tonight," I told him.

"Thank you and you're looking good enough to eat," he

BREANNA J.

said.

I turned around in a circle, smiling, "Thank you."

"So, what are you doing in a place like this?" he asked.

"I'm having a girls' night out," I told him and sipped my drink.

"Oh, like a bachelorette party?" he asked.

"Yeah, something like that I guess you can say. But, what are you doing here?" I asked him.

"A few of the fellas wanted to step out tonight so I'm here with them," he answered back.

"Mmhm," I said as I took another sip.

"So, why haven't you called me back so we can arrange a time to meet up?" he asked me.

"We're meeting right now," I laughed as I started to walk away.

Tony grabbed my arm.

I looked him in the eyes and then down at his hand gripping my arm. Without me having to say nothing, Tony let go.

"Sasha, I just want to talk to you. Keyz is my boy, but you deserve better. Ever since we met that night, you're all I think about. Before you get married, just let me take you out

In The Name of Love

one time. If you feel nothing, then so be it, but I got to at least try. My heart won't let me rest until I know I gave my best effort."

I looked at Tony and then walked off and rejoined the girls.

Tony and his boy walked past our table and he stared at me with every step he took.

"Sasha, ain't that the fine ass cop from the shop?" Katrina asked.

I sipped my drink.

"Yup, that's him."

We enjoyed the rest of the night. We laughed and we danced. Kim twerked and made more money than the strippers. We all took turns buying a round for everyone. We were definitely lit. Our table had bad bitches and the baddest strippers, which brought some of the hottest niggas over. We were the center of attention.

I tapped Kim on her shoulder while she was getting a lap dance and told her, "I'm going to the bathroom. Watch my drink."

She nodded her head and I walked off.

I went to the bathroom. As I washed my hands, Trisha came into the bathroom and stood behind me.

BREANNA J.

"Did you think about my offer?" she asked me.

"I did," I answered.

"So, what are you going to do?" she asked me with a curious face.

I said nothing for a minute.

She looked at me, waiting for an answer.

I smiled at her and said, "I'm not into girls, but for you I might be. I guess you'll have to wait to the end of the night to find out."

I walked past Trish and out of the bathroom. Trish stood there watching every step I took until the bathroom door closed.

I went back to the table and joined the party. We danced the rest of the night away. I felt like I had my swag back. I had been tripping over one nigga that was doing me wrong, but in one night alone, I had a man and a woman on me.

Shit, I was that bitch tonight. This was the type of fun and lifestyle I had been missing deep down inside.

When the night was over, we all headed out to our cars. We stood outside talking and I told everyone that no one was driving tonight. We were all too drunk. We all agreed and pulled out our phones to order Ubers. Some guys walked by. They were talking out the side of their neck telling us that we

In The Name of Love

didn't need Uber that they'd take us home, but we ignored them all.

As I told Kim how far away the Uber was, Tony chimed in from behind me.

"Sasha, I'll take you to get food so you can sober up. Then, I will take you home to Keyz if you'd like."

I turned around and looked at him.

This man was something else.

"Nah, I'm good. My man wouldn't like or appreciate any man dropping me off to his home, but I'm sure you know that already seeing that he is your boy. Plus, I already got a ride. Trish and I are getting an Uber together."

As I said it, Trish looked up at me in shock. In all honesty, I was shocked too. I wasn't sure what the hell I was doing, but as of right now, I was blaming it on the liquor and the fact that Keyz was ignoring me.

I thought to myself, *What in the hell did I just sign myself up for?*

I looked at Tony.

He walked away and left me alone.

BREANNA J.

Chapter Sixteen

We waited for the Uber to come for Kim and the rest of the ladies.

Once we knew that everyone was safely on their way home, Trish turned to me and asked, "Are you ready?"

I looked at her.

"Are you driving or getting an Uber?"

Trisha assured me she was good enough to drive.

So, I looked at my phone one more time just to see if Keyz was hitting my phone or checking to see where I was.

I called his phone. It rung and rung until it eventually went to voicemail. That showed me how concerned he was about me.

"Fuck it, let's go," I said as I walked over to Trish's car.

Trisha got in the car and looked at me.

"Are you sure about this?" she asked me.

I looked at her.

"Why are you asking me that, are you scared?" I asked her.

IN THE NAME OF LOVE

"Baby girl, I am far from scared, but I know that this is something different for you. I just want to make sure you've thought this all the way through," she said.

I rubbed on Trisha's thighs and said, "Let's go."

Trisha drove us to her house. She lived in this really nice looking apartment building. She parked and led me up to her apartment on the fifth floor. The apartment was really sexy and modern day classy. Everything was black and white and she had tons of windows looking out to the city.

Trisha told me to get comfortable, so I had a seat on her couch while she went into the kitchen.

She came out with a drink and handed it to me.

"Do you want something to eat?" she asked me.

I shook my head and told her, "Nah, I'm good."

Trisha sat down on the couch next to me and looked at me.

"You're really beautiful, you know that?"

I blushed.

"Thank you."

Trisha pulled my feet up on her lap and unzipped my boots. She began to rub my feet.

I relaxed and thanked her.

BREANNA J.

Trisha rubbed my feet and then started to make her way up my legs to my thighs. The way Trish was touching my body had my pussy jumping and getting super wet. It was as if I could feel my heartbeat in my vagina.

I had never looked at a girl in a sexual way and honestly I was scared. I had never stepped out on Keyz, but Trish had my body desiring her. I was ready to let Trish have her way with me and whatever happened, well, it just happened.

I looked around.

"So, what happens now?" I asked her.

Trisha got up and took my hand. She led me to her bedroom. She told me to turn around and she unzipped my jumpsuit while kissing on my neck and shoulders, then every bit of my back and body that she released. When the jumpsuit finally fell to the ground, I stepped out of it and turned around to face her while cupping my breasts with my hands.

Trisha looked at me.

"I can't kiss on them and taste them if you're holding on to them," she said with a smirk.

I dropped my hands and Trish gently caressed my breasts. She played with my nipples. Then, she licked them.

"Lay on the bed," she said to me in a sexy tone of voice.

Trish got undressed and I must say I thought her body was banging with the clothes on, but those clothes did her body no justice. When she took those pants off, it seemed as if her ass grew twice as big and with the corset removed. Her breasts looked like she had double D's on her chest and the little stomach pudge she had fit her shape.

Trisha stood in front of me in a red thong and red strapless bra. She crawled on the bed, kissing from my feet to my lips as she got into the bed. Once she was next to me, she rubbed on my breast more. She also sucked and kissed on them. It felt so good. Then, she kissed me. The kiss was so gentle, pure and passionate. From my lips, she worked her way back to my breasts. She licked and sucked on them just right. She even did this thing with her tongue that got my nipples so hard and my panties so wet. The more she kept going, the wetter I got.

Trish went from holding my breast up to her mouth to sucking with no hands. Her hands traveled down my stomach and rubbed on my thighs. She separated my legs and then guided her hand up to my vagina. She rubbed on it through my panties as she looked me in my eyes.

"You like that?" she asked softly.

I bit my bottom lip as Trish brought her hand to the top of my panties and then inside of them.

She made her way right to the clit and rubbed on it gently, but at the same time, she was aggressive enough for me to feel her.

"It feels so good" I moaned.

BREANNA J.

Trish smirked and started kissing down my body to my thighs. I was so turned on and ready. I couldn't take the teasing any more.

I started to lift my pelvis off the bed to give her hints to take my panties off.

She looked up at me.

"Oh, you're ready, huh?' Trish asked me with a smirk on her face.

She slid my panties down.

"Damn, it's just as pretty as I thought it would be," Trisha said as she went into kiss my thighs.

Trisha rolled her tongue from the inside of my thighs up to my vagina. She used her hand and separated my pussy lips apart. As she teased me the feeling of her tongue on my clit made me even wetter. Then, she sucked on my clit. It felt so good that I let out a moan. As she sucked on my clit, she slid her fingers inside of me.

I let out an exhale.

Trish took her mouth off my pussy just long enough to say, "Damn, you taste good! Your pussy is tight and it's warm. Not to mention super wet."

I pushed her face back down. This felt too good for her to fuck up my nut by talking.

In The Name of Love

I let Trisha finger fuck me as she ate my pussy. I got to the point of almost climaxing and then I pushed her away.

Trish got close to me and whispered to me, "Let it happen, you'll feel better."

Trish licked her fingers that she just had inside of me and looked at me seductively. I was sure that she was letting me know that liked the taste. She slid them fingers back in, rubbed my clit with her thumb and sucked on my nipple.

I went to try to move her hand, but she pinned both of my hands above my head.

"But I'm about to cum," I said out loud.

"Good," she said.

The more she kept going and the better the feeling got, I started to drift into a happy place. Before I knew it, I was cumming all over Trish's hand.

She smiled as she licked my juices from her fingers.

I moved to the end of Trish's bed and reached for my clothes while she turned to look in her nightstand.

"What are you doing? I'm not done with you yet," she said when she saw me starting to put my legs into my pants.

She pulled a strap-on out her nightstand and sat it on the bed.

BREANNA J.

"I'm not with that. Keyz will feel the difference and think I was fucking some nigga."

Trish's face frowned up a little.

"Okay fine, come here then," she said as she put the strap-on away.

I walked around the bed to where she was and stood there.

She laid back on the bed.

"Come here," she said.

"I'm here," I told her.

"Nah, come here," she said, pointing to her mouth.

I looked at her sideways.

"Really? Right there?" I asked her.

"Yes, I need you to nut one more time for me before you go home to him," she replied back to me.

I climbed on to the bed and then sat on Trish's face. The operator might have been a little different, but I definitely knew how to ride this ride. I rode Trish's face until I had nothing left for her to taste.

In The Name of Love

Chapter Seventeen

I would have never expected my straight ass to be laying next to a female butt naked and fully satisfied after she had just damn near took my soul.

I looked over and Trish was knocked out.

I eased out of bed and grabbed my shoes and clothes. I got dressed in her living room and then wrote Trish a note right before I slipped out the front door.

Thanks for the amazing time. Text me at (617)777-8285 I feel like I owe you lunch.

Sasha

As I waited for the elevator to get to Trisha's floor, I pulled my phone out. I had missed calls and text from Katrina and Kim letting me know that they were home safe and asking whether I was good. There was not one text or missed call from Keyz.

When the elevator doors opened, I opened up my Uber app and put my current location and the address to Pearl. I stood in the lobby and waited for my ride to arrive.

My Uber pulled up and I hopped in, heading to the club to get my car.

As I rode to my car, I looked out the window and thought to myself, *I just cheated on Keyz.*

BREANNA J.

I was just as wrong as he was. I had to be honest and tell him, but then again, it was only sex and with a female. I didn't stay the night with her. I didn't spend money on here, and there was a long past that I knew about that he didn't.

When I got to my car and hopped in, I noticed a rose and note stuck to my windshield.

I got out and opened the note.

Your actions tonight were cute and turned me on a little bit. Because I know if you would ride for him that hard, with the man that I am you would go even harder for me.

Tony

I sat in my car and looked at the note. I smelled the rose. Then, I threw the note out the window and pulled off.

When I got to my house, it was silent. Keyz's car and bike was here, but I didn't hear any TV's on or snoring.

I stood at the bottom of the steps, trying to determine if I should go get in bed or not. I decided to go in the den and sleep on the couch that way Keyz would never what time I actually came in. He would just think I was too drunk to climb up the stairs. This way, I wouldn't be getting in bed dirty and smelling like sex.

I dozed off on the couch and it felt like the best sleep I had gotten in a while.

Around nine, I was awakened to the sound of Keyz com-

IN THE NAME OF LOVE

ing in the house.

I walked out the den.

When I walked into the kitchen, Keyz was yelling in the phone, "Fix it and fix it now or that's everyone's ass."

That didn't matter to me because I had heard him threaten people before. What actually caught my attention was that he still had on the same clothes he had on yesterday.

I leaned against the doorway of the kitchen and said, "Hello to you, too."

Keyz turned around and looked as if he had seen a ghost.

"Baby, what you doing here?"

I looked at Keyz with the side eye.

"Keyz, I live here. What do you mean what am I doing here?"

Keyz walked towards me and wrapped his arms around me. He kissed my forehead.

"Not like that. You know what I mean," he said.

I looked at Keyz and said, "Nah, I don't know what you mean."

He smiled and laughed "Relax, I just meant I would have expected you to still be with the girls. You know, maybe sleep

BREANNA J.

at one of their houses after all the fun y'all had at Pearl last night."

I backed up from Keyz.

"How do you know where I was last night?' I asked him.

"Sasha baby, there is nowhere you can go that I won't know about," he said to me.

I folded my arms.

"Well, if you knew where I was last night, why didn't your ass answer the phone when I called?"

Keyz looked away when I asked him that so I knew the next thing to come out his mouth was going to be a lie.

"Bae, I was busy," he said.

"Oh, you were busy? Is that why you got on the same clothes from yesterday? And why are you just getting in the house at nine in the morning? The sun should not be beating you home, Keyz!" I let him know with an attitude.

Keyz giggled a little, which made me madder.

"Keyz, don't play with me today," I said to him.

"I was out handling some stuff that don't involve you and isn't worth being placed in your beautiful head."

I mushed Keyz.

IN THE NAME OF LOVE

"What the fuck? Your ass ain't ever have any secrets you kept from me before, besides your little bitches. So, what the fuck was you doing? Were you cheating? If so, cool, I don't care! Get it out of your system so that when we say I do you can be fuckin' faithful!" I said as I mushed him again.

Keyz turned and walked towards the fridge while he said, "Sasha, I'm not hiding shit and I am not cheating. It's just that some stuff is better for you not to know, damn. That way if you ever get pulled into a police station over some shit I did or supposedly did, you can say that you don't know and it'll be true."

As I got ready to say something back to Keyz, my phone started to ring in the den. I stood there staring at Keyz for a few moments before walking off to go get the phone.

"Hello," I said when I answered.

"Hello, this is Officer Nicholas Murry with the police department. May I speak to Sasha?"

"Ugh, this is she," I groaned, hoping that he caught on to my disapproval of him calling me.

"Sasha, I'm not sure if you remember, but we spoke before. I am calling you again because I am the head Detective on your brother's case. You are listed as his only living relative outside of Calvin Sr, who is in Florida. Every time I try to reach out to him, I get no answer.

"As I told you before, it's been two years since my brother's death and I am not reopening that door again. And just so

BREANNA J.

you know, the reason Calvin Sr. isn't returning your calls is because there is nothing he can tell you about his son. He left us when I was 2 and CJ was 5, so please do not call me again unless you have someone arrested for my brother's death!"

By this time I was screaming and didn't realize it.

Keyz was standing next to me.

"I understand a death is something no one wants to re-live, but I would truly like to meet with you about some new information that was brought to us. I think that we are getting close to finding your brother's killer," he pressed.

"No, and don't call me anymore like I said!" I screamed.

I hung up.

My heart was racing and my anger was past the level of pissed.

Keyz walked up and hugged me. Being in his arms made the tears stream down my face.

"Baby, talk to me. What's going on with you? You're walking around snapping and not being yourself. Are you okay?" Keyz asked.

I screamed, "I am tired of everything. I'm tired of people bothering me and I have to just take it. I'm tired of the games and lies. Now, on top of everything else I got going on, I got the police calling my phone, trying to have me help them reopen CJ's case."

In The Name of Love

Keyz stood and looked at me. He let me get everything out that I had been holding on to.

Once I was done and breathing heavy from all the yelling, Keyz reached out and wiped my face.

"Sasha baby, why didn't you tell me all this was going on? I am your man. I am here to support you, help you and protect you, but I can't do that if you're bottling everything up inside. I am your soon to be husband. There are no more other women. I am here for you. But, I can't be unless you tell me what's going on. You don't have to hold on to this shit, let me carry the load," he said to me.

I couldn't tell if Keyz was trying to butter me up or being real with me, but he was saying what I needed to hear.

I sat on the couch and cried out the rest of the tears I had inside.

"Bae, get dressed, let's go wedding shopping," Keyz said.

I wiped my tears.

"That's nice but I have to get to my clients," I said to him as I got up and got ready to walk out the den.

"Cancel your clients. Tell them you don't feel good and come with your man," he said back to me as he got ready to walk off.

"Keyz, that's losing out on money."

BREANNA J.

Keyz turned around and gave me an annoyed look. Then, he walked to the small closet we had in the den and pulled out his duffle bag that he carried when he was going to play basketball. Keyz walked over to the couch with the bag and unzipped it. The bag was full of money that I had never seen or even knew was in my house. He took out of two stacks of money. Both of the stacks were tied with rubber bands. Then, he slammed it on the couch next to him.

"Will this cover the money you'll be missing out on? Damn."

I picked up the money and smiled.

"This looks like it will do."

Keyz zipped the bag up. He laughed and stood up.

"You're such a brat. Now, don't you ever talk that money talk to me again when I ask you to do something," he said as he kissed me.

"Ummm, but bae, where did that money come from?" I asked Keyz.

Keyz looked at me.

"Promise, you won't get mad if I tell you, Sasha?" he said.

I sucked my teeth.

"Promise. Now, tell me."

In The Name of Love

"Well when CJ died, his turf was up for grabs, so I took it. I provided them with product and ever since I've been taking that money I make and stashing it in different places just in case we ever needed it."

I walked out the den and headed towards the stairs.

Keyz followed me.

"Sasha?"

I turned around and looked at him.

"Yes?" I answered.

Keyz looked at me as if he were a kid that knew they had just did something wrong.

"Are you mad at me?"

I turned around on the stairs and said, "No hun, I'm going to go get dressed."

I continued up the stairs.

I went into our room and sat at the edge of the bed. I looked at the money Keyz had just gave me. I shook my head.

At least, he came clean about something, I thought to myself.

I went into the bathroom and turned on the shower. As I showered, I flashed back to the night I had just spent with

BREANNA J.

Trish.

     Every part of my body that I washed reminded me of the way that she touched me, kissed me and sucked on me. I knew what I did was wrong, but at least I had done it before we were married. I had to see what I was missing out on by being only with Keyz. That way I would have no desire to step out while we are married.

     I showered and came out. I could hear Keyz showering in the bathroom in the hallway. I started getting dressed and he walked in the room with a towel wrapped around him. Water was dripping off of him and his dreads were pulled up.

     We both got dressed and headed downstairs. Keyz got a phone call and went in the den while I went into the kitchen to grab a yogurt. Once I had my yogurt, I tried to stand outside the den to see if I could hear what Keyz was talking about without him seeing me. All I got was "Fuckin' find her" and then he slammed the phone on the desk we had in the den.

     I went in the den with a smile on my face as if I had heard nothing.

     "Let's go bae, and grab some more of that money you had stashed because I'm about to make you ball out. I need new luggage, and I want us to have matching outfits, and you need new boxers, and I want the wedding party to have shirts with their role on them. Not to mention, I want to bring goodie bags to give everyone and we find my dress" I listed off to him as I put on my shades and grabbed my purse while heading to the door.

In The Name of Love

Keyz just stood there and smiled at me.

I turned around and pulled my shades down so I could look over them at him.

"What's wrong? Why are you not moving?" I asked him.

"Nothing is wrong, bae; I was just admiring the joy I see you have about this wedding. This is the first time since you said yes to marrying me that I actually seen you happy to do something for the wedding."

I stopped and smiled.

"Come on now because I need to shop for you, too. You will not be in my wedding pictures with the ugly sandals that every uncle wears to the family barbecue with the socks."

We both laughed.

"Let's go, crazy girl," he said as he grabbed his car keys.

BREANNA J.

Chapter Eighteen

We went out and got into Keyz's car. He drove and I sat on the passenger side, looking cute and cracking jokes. It reminded me of old times. We were laughing, talking and singing along to the best of the 90s R&B on Pandora.

I turned the music down while Keyz was all into Jodeci's "Come and Talk to me."

"Bae, so what should our wedding song be?" I asked him.

Keyz looked at me and said, "Let's Get it On" by Marvin Gaye."

We both laughed.

"Shut up and be serious. What should our song be?" I asked him.

Keyz sat in silence for a few moments while we waited for the light to turn green.

Then finally he said, "This might sound corny, but I want to see you walk down to Jamie Foxx's 'Wedding Vows.' That song describes my love for you, Sasha."

"Really?" I asked him.

"Yes, let me play it for you."

I sat and listened to the song. It was so meaningful. I

IN THE NAME OF LOVE

couldn't believe that Keyz even listened to something like this.

As the song ended, I sat there stuck and in a daze until my phone buzzed in my purse. It was the shop calling.

"Hello?" I answered.

"Hey Sasha, its Tasha. No one is here at the shop, besides me. I called Katrina and she's not answering. Are you coming in today?" she asked.

"No, I'm not feeling too well. I'm staying home. I got two clients this afternoon, can you call them and reschedule for me?" I instructed.

"Sure, no problem," she said.

"Thanks hun, I'll call Katrina and see what's going on with her," I told her.

She said alright and then we both hung up.

When I hung up, I noticed that I had a text.

I opened it:

I woke up and you had snuck out and left me a note. Hope you enjoyed yourself. When is the next time you want to get together?

I read the text and then looked over at Keyz. He was in his own world, driving and jamming to the music.

BREANNA J.

I texted Trish back quickly.

Sorry for sneaking out. I had to get home. I did enjoy myself; thank you once again. But I don't think there will be a next time. I will just have to live with the memories of how good you made me feel.

I sent the message and then deleted the whole text thread from my phone. I put my phone back in my purse and went back to giving my attention to Keyz. I sat there in the passenger seat just staring at him.

We pulled up to a building I hadn't been to before.

"What's here?" I asked Keyz.

"This is the travel agent's place. We got to pick up the tickets," Keyz answered me.

I got out the car and went in the building. The travel agent gave us everyone's ticket, boarding info and anything else we might need for this trip. Right before we got ready to walk out her office, she handed us a basket that read: *congrats Mr. and Mrs.* It was so odd to know I was this close to being a married woman.

We got back in the car and my phone started to go off. I pulled it out and it was a text. I expected it to be another text from Trish or one from Kim or Katrina.

Instead when I opened it, it read.

I hope you got my rose and the note I left you on your

IN THE NAME OF LOVE

car.

I didn't even bother to text back.

I put the phone back in my purse and asked Keyz "So, where are we going now?"

Keyz shrugged his shoulder and then asked, "Do you have a dress in mind that you want?" Keyz asked.

"No," I said back quickly.

"Why not? I thought you and the girls were going to go take a look. Do you want to go now? " Keyz asked me.

I looked at Keyz.

"Because my mom and CJ aren't here. A mom is supposed to help a daughter pick out her wedding dress, and although CJ wasn't my dad, he was the closest thing I had to one and he was supposed to walk me down to you," I said to him as I put my head down.

Keyz reached over and put his hand under my chin to raise my head.

"I'll go with you and share the moment with you. When you put on that dress and walk down to me in Jamaica, I promise I will still think you're just as beautiful in that moment as the first time I saw you."

I smiled.

BREANNA J.

Keyz really did try to be there for me a lot. I had to give him credit for that.

"No baby, I'll do it with Kim. I want the first time you see me in my wedding dress to be when we stand before the Lord and our friends and say our vows," I said to him as I rubbed the hand he had resting on my face.

IN THE NAME OF LOVE

Chapter Nineteen

Keyz nodded his head and turn forward. He put the car in drive.

As we drove around, I asked, "Keyz, can I ask you a question?"

"Yeah, what's up shorty?" he answered, smiling.

"Why aren't your mom and dad coming to see their son get married?" I asked.

I quickly seen the smile leave Keyz's face. It was almost like Keyz had seen a ghost.

Keyz pulled over.

"What do you know about my parents?" he asked.

I wasn't sure if he was angry or in fear. We had never talked about his parents before. The only reason I even knew they were alive or what their names were was because I had seen Keyz's birth certificate one day and took a look at it. After, I looked at it, my Inspector Gadget ass went and looked them up.

"I know that they are alive," I told him.

"Okay, why are you asking about them, though?" he questioned.

BREANNA J.

"Because bae we are getting married and I'd like to know if my mother in law or father in law even approve or like me," I responded back to him.

Keyz took a deep breath.

"Me inviting them is like you inviting Calvin Sr. At this point in my life, I am not 100% sure if they are dead or alive or where to find them. My mom was a cocaine addict and my dad was her dealer. My dad didn't want anything to do with me or her once she told him she was pregnant, but he kept selling her drugs. By the time I was 10, my mom had sniffed so much crack that she owed my dad thousands of dollars. To pay him off, she traded me to him to work off her debt."

"Once I completely paid off my mom's debit, I ran away to live with my grandma on my mom's side. I was fifteen, and neither of them came looking for me. I learned how to lie about my age and how to make it on my own. So, in my head I never had parents. Six months after my grandma Jenny died, I came here," Keyz told me.

"So, Jenny is your grandma. I thought that name tattooed on your arm was short for Jennifer, your mother's name," I told him, shocked.

"Nope, Jenny is my grandma and the only family I had," Keyz told me.

It felt so odd to know that I didn't know any of this about the man I had been lying next to for years. These were things that made him who he was and I didn't know it.

IN THE NAME OF LOVE

"Do you know if you have brothers or sisters?" I asked him.

"My mom had two other kids before me. Toya and Kevin. but she lost them to the system. It's said that my father has an unknown number of kids running around," Keyz answered.

"Bae, why have you never told me any of this? We could have been trying to find your siblings and build your family," I let him know.

"Because my siblings aren't lost. Toya is in a mental hospital. My mom did so many drugs while pregnant with her that she came out with mental problems. When she went into the system, she went from foster home to group home. Her last foster father was raping her and when she couldn't take any more, she stabbed him. Because she was mentally unstable, they locked her away in a mental hospital."

As for Kevin, he was serving a life sentence in a prison up north for a supposed killing he did. But he was killed a year ago in a prison riot. They don't know who did it or what they used to stab him. All they know is that the riot happened and by time they got all the inmates calmed down and in their cell, Kevin was dead," Keyz finished.

All I could do was sit in shock. Keyz never talked about his family so I would have never known this was going on. I would have never in a million years imagined this was what he was dealing with.

"Well baby, we have each other now, and in a matter of days, we will be a legal family," I said to him.

BREANNA J.

Keyz put the car back in drive and we finished the errands we had to run. We gathered the papers from the courthouse to sign with the pastor that was going to marry us. We got wine to put in the thank you baskets I wanted to make for Kim, Tasha, Sean and Katrina to thank them for coming to our wedding. Then, we headed home to pack and put everything together.

As I sat on my couch looking at my man put stuff into our luggage, it finally hit me. I was days away from marrying my Mr. Just Right for Me.

We had come a long way.

It was 7 P.M. at night and he was home with me; he was not looking at his phone or getting ready to rush out. This was the beginning of something great. We had made it through so much and I knew there was so much happiness on the way. This was meant to be. This was our happily ever after.

In The Name of Love

Chapter Twenty

The time had went by so fast. It was finally time to go to Jamaica. In a matter of a few hours, I would be boarding a plane and on my way to being Mrs. Shaw. I couldn't be happier. Things had been going so good. I was glowing and Keyz was looking more and more handsome every day.

Kim had went on a date with Simone, but since then she had disappeared. She wasn't answering her phone. Even Trish aid it had been a while since she seen her sister. But, that she was known for disappearing when she didn't get her way. I guess she finally realized my man didn't want her and moved on.

As I sat on the edge of my bed my phone rang.

I rolled over.

Keyz wasn't there, so I answered the phone.

"Hello?" I said.

"Hello gorgeous," Trish said.

"Hey Trish." I said.

"Did you get the flowers I sent you yesterday?" she asked me.

"Yeah I got them, they came to the shop. Thank you so much."

BREANNA J.

"Good, I saw them and thought they were just as beautiful as you," she complimented.

I blushed.

Although me and Trish hadn't done anything since our first encounter, we still texted and talked all the time. She was good company, even though sometimes she tried to convince me to let her get another taste. I would normally laugh it off and tell her no. As a answer to my rejection, she'd tell me I was scared.

"So, today's the day," she said.

"Well it's not *the* day, but yeah, I'm leaving for Jamaica today," I said.

"I still think you should leave him and get with me," she said into the phone, almost sounding like she had an attitude.

"You know how I feel about Keyz, so that's not even an option. Just be happy for me and be my friend, Trish," I said to her sincerely.

"Ugh, okay I guess. But, when he fucks up, just know I'm here," she said.

I laughed.

"Bye, girl. I'ma text you later. I got to get ready."

I hung up and sat there thinking about what Trish had just said. Honestly in the back of my mind, the only reason I still

IN THE NAME OF LOVE

had her around was because if Keyz started to act up and I needed to bust a nut, I wouldn't feel as bad if it was from her instead of another man. I mean it's not really cheating because she was a female.

I got up and headed into the bathroom. As I washed my face and brushed my teeth, I dialed Kim's number and put the phone in speaker.

She answered the phone super excited.

"Hey, Ms. Shaw to be!"

"Hey boo. Are you ready?"

"Yes. I'm all packed and my bags are next to the door. My ticket is in my purse. Are you ready? Are you nervous?"

I answered, "Yes I am, and yes, for some reason I feel like I got to throw up."

"Well, get your nerves together sissy so we can get on this plane."

"I am, you just don't forget my dress," I reminded her.

"I would never. I have it ready to go."

"Okay. Sean should be there to pick you up soon. I'll see you at the airport."

"Alright, see you then."

BREANNA J.

I had given my dress to Kim because I didn't want to bring it home and risk Keyz seeing it. After Keyz offered to take me dress shopping, I knew it was time to get to the store, so I got the girls together and we went. I fell in love with this Vera Wang dress from her summer collection. It had a mermaid bottom going into a long train. And of course I had to be extra and get the dress that had sequins and rhinestones on it. When I came out in it, the girls all cried at how beautiful I looked in it. When I finally got to the mirror in the store, I cried as well when I saw myself.

Keyz came in the bathroom.

"Good morning, beautiful," he said with a smile.

"Good morning, my handsome soon to be husband."

I smiled back at Keyz.

Keyz walked over and gave me a kiss.

I pushed past him and rushed to the toilet to throw up.

"Bae, you good?" he asked.

"Yes it's just my nerves. I'll be good. Did you get everything packed? I told Kim Sean was coming to get her. Did you text him and remind him?" I asked.

"Yes baby, everything is packed and going fine. Is there anything I can do for you right now to make you feel better?" Keyz asked.

In The Name of Love

"No, I'm fine I'm about to get dressed," I told Keyz.

Keyz walked off and I got up and ready for the day right along with him.

By the time I was completely dressed, Keyz was already downstairs and had taken our luggage to the car. I came downstairs and stared at my man. He was looking good; real GQ style with his shades on, dreads pulled back, and a short sleeve linen outfit.

I was matching his fly. I had on a black casual sundress, black Chanel sandals and a matching Chanel bag and sunglasses.

"You ready?" I asked when I got to the last stair.

"Yes, let's go," Keyz turned to me and took my hand as he said it.

.I looked around my house that we had built together. We were leaving here dating. In a week when we returned, we would be living together married.

We got in the car and drove to the airport. We met our wedding party at the front door and we got checked in. We made sure that everything was in order.

Keyz handed out all the tickets and we went through security. There was no issue. We all made it to the plane boarding gate and were overly excited to get this trip started. There was an hour delay with the plane, so the men decided to go to the bar that was a few gates down and have a beer.

BREANNA J.

Me and the girls sat at the gate and talked.

Kim said, "Sasha, thank you so much for bringing me on this trip with you."

Yes, thank you Sasha," Candy and Tasha said together.

"No, thank you ladies for stepping away from your lives and coming. And thank Keyz for paying for it all," I said.

We all laughed.

"Are you nervous?" Kim asked.

"Yes, very! I woke up and threw up this morning."

"Really? Eww," Candy said.

Candy gave me a side eye.

"Yes, as a matter of fact, I kind of feel like I need to throw up again now," I admitted.

I got up and walked towards the bathroom. Kim followed behind me. Once I got into the bathroom, everything I had in me came right out into the airport toilet.

Kim stood outside the stall and asked, "Sasha, are you sure you good enough to get on this plane? This seems like more than nerves," she pointed out.

I opened the stall door.

In The Name of Love

"Yes Kim, I am fine,"

Kim just looked at me.

"What Kim, damn?"

Kim looked at me with a concerned look on her face.

"Do you think you may be pregnant?" she asked me.

I blurted out quick, "No, I can't be. I'm just sick. If I was pregnant, I would know."

As me and Kim stood in the bathroom talking, we heard them call over the loud speaker that our flight was finally preparing to board.

I wiped my face and cleaned myself up. Kim gave me a stick of game to freshen up my breath and we went out to the gate. As we were walking back, we could see the guys were heading back to the gate as well.

We all boarded the plane. Keyz sat next to me and as we settling in for takeoff, he looked at me.

"What's wrong bae, are you good?" he asked.

I smiled.

"I am perfectly fine. We are on our way to having a beautiful wedding with my handsome man," I said as I gave him a kiss.

BREANNA J.

Keyz relaxed and the flight attendant came out and did her speech. Before we knew it, we were off. Keyz drifted off and I was there staring out the window. I replayed the conversation me and Kim had. Me, pregnant? Someone's mother? Me and Keyz actually having a family? So many thing flashed before my eyes. Me in labor and the look on Keyz's face as he held our first child for the first time.

So many things had crossed my mind that I didn't hear the flight attendant asking if I wanted something off her cart to drink.

"Ma'am excuse me… Miss, ma'am can I get you something?" the flight attendant asked.

"Oh, my gosh, I am so sorry. Yes, can I get a ginger ale for me and for him a jack and coke with no ice? He'll drink it when he wakes up," I told her.

She gave me the drinks and went off to the next person.

I got up and squeezed past Keyz, rushing to the bathroom. On my way to the bathroom, I saw Sean and Kim were sitting next to each other. They were laughing and talking. I didn't know if that was a good or bad thing and at the moment. I didn't have time to question them about it because I had to throw up.

When I came out the restroom, Kim was standing at the door.

"You good?" she asked.

167

IN THE NAME OF LOVE

"Yeah, my stomach is just still messed up," I told her.

"Or, you're pregnant Sasha, just face it," she said back to me with an attitude.

I looked at Kim.

"Yo, stop saying that before someone hears you. I'm not pregnant. Anyway, what the hell is going on with you and Sean? Y'all sure look buddy buddy," I said back to her.

"Ugh, Sasha. Nothing, we're just talking and being friendly. He's a cool guy and he's sexy."

I looked at her.

"Okay, be careful. He's a baby maker."

We laughed.

"It's not even that type of party. I am just trying to enjoy this trip."

Kim started to walk back to her seat and I followed her. Then, I stopped in my footsteps and went back to the bathroom.

BREANNA J.

Chapter Twenty-One

Once the flight landed, we all got our bags and headed to the shuttle Keyz had set up for us. When we got to hotel, I was memorized. Keyz had went all the way out with this place. There was a beautiful lobby, pool and the people were so nice and friendly.

When we got up to the room, it was like a fairytale. This four bedroom suite was to die for. Katrina and Candy decided to share a room, which left a room for me and Keyz, and Sean and Kim to have their own room.

We were all pretty tired and a little jet lagged after the 12 hour flight. So once the rooms was assigned, we went to our rooms and went to bed. Keyz and I laid in bed and just looked at each other.

"Sasha, you're going to be my wife in less than 48 hours," he said with this cheesy smile on his face.

I looked at him in silence.

"Sasha?" he said to get my attention.

"Yes?" I answered him.

"What's on your mind? Talk to me. You've been so quit and to yourself all day," he said to me.

I looked him in the face.

IN THE NAME OF LOVE

"I'm good baby, I'm just admiring the fact that we are really here and doing this," I said to him.

We kissed and Keyz said, "Yes, we are really here. I am this much closer to locking you down, girl," he said to me.

We laughed as he pulled me closer to his chest. I was so at peace and we both drifted off to sleep.

We woke up the next morning to the smell of bacon and food cooking. I rolled over and Keyz wasn't in bed. Now, it was one thing for us to be back home and him not being in bed with me when I woke up, but in Jamaica, there was no other place he should be besides in bed with me.

I got up, grabbed my robe and went out to the living room of the suite.

Katrina and Tasha were in the kitchen cooking.

"Good morning ladies," I said.

They both turned around and smiled.

"Good morning," they said at once.

"Do you ladies need any help?" I asked as I leaned over the counter to see what they were making.

"No we are good, we are almost done," Katrina said.

"Ok, well I have so much planned for us to do today, so I hope you ladies are excited and ready," I said to them.

BREANNA J.

"I'm ready for whatever you got planned," Katrina said.

She took a sip of her drink.

"So we are going to let the guys do whatever they wanted while we go have us a girls day. We are going to going to get facials, pedicures, manicures, massages, and of course, we'll go shopping. And drum roll… it's all on my man."

We all laughed.

"Poor Keyz is going to be broke when this trip is over," Tasha said.

"Girl he makes money for me to spend, and he always has a stash somewhere. Not to mention, when he dies, he can't take it with him."

We all laughed some more.

"Well, I'm down," Tasha said.

"Me too," Katrina agreed.

"Well, can we get down to this food? " I asked.

"Yeah, get everyone else," Katrina said. "

Where is everyone? Because Keyz is not in our room," I said.

"We don't know, but if they don't come on, we will be

IN THE NAME OF LOVE

eating without them," Katrina said.

"Let me go find them," I offered.

I went to Kim's room and knocked on her door. There was no answer. I opened the door and there was no Kim.

Now, where could her little ass be?

I went to Sean's room. I did the same to him and when I opened his room door, there was no sign of him, but yet I could hear him.

"Yo Sean, you in here?" I yelled out into his room.

The bathroom door opened.

"What's up?" Sean said as he peeked his head out the door.

"Nigga, it's time to eat. Have you seen Kim and Keyz?" I asked.

Sean opened the bathroom door and said, "Yeah, Kim is right here."

Kim was sitting on the sink's countertop.

"Hey Sash'," she said when we locked eyes.

"Hey my ass, what the hell are you doing in the bathroom with this nigga?" I questioned her with anger in my eyes.

BREANNA J.

"Chill Sasha, it ain't even like that," Sean said. "I just wanted to smoke and I asked her to join me."

Kim jumped off the counter and walked towards me.

"Mmm, where the hell did y'all get the weed from anyway? I know y'all didn't get on the plane with that shit," I said, looking at them both.

Sean responded, "Hell nah, that would have been stupid trying to get on the plane with some loud. I got connects here."

I just looked at Sean.

"Man, y'all get dressed and come out here and eat. Tasha and Katrina cooked," I said, walking out the room. "Oh Sean where the fuck is Keyz?" I asked, turning around.

Tasha yelled out from the kitchen, "He just went in y'all room."

I walked in the living room with an angry face.

"What's wrong with you?" Candy asked.

"Nothing just need to go to the bathroom, I'll be back out and Pookie and Kim should be coming out," I said.

"Okay, you sure you're okay?" Katrina asked with a little concern in her voice.

"Yes, I'm fine. My nerves are just getting the best of me,"

IN THE NAME OF LOVE

I said, blowing off her concern a little as I walked into the room.

I walked in the room and Keyz was out on the balcony.

I went to the bathroom and sat on the edge of the tub in front of the toilet. I felt like I had to throw up but nothing was coming out. Time had passed and I had repeatedly tried to leave the bathroom, but turned around thinking it was finally coming up.

As I sat on the floor of the bathroom, I heard Keyz come in talking on the phone.

"Find that bitch and you better find her before I get back. Pregnant bitches just don't disappear. If you don't get this handled before I get back, I'm going to kill her and you," e harshly said in to the phone.

I waited a few minutes and then I brushed my teeth and walked out the bathroom.

"Good morning, handsome," I said to him.

Keyz turned around and said, "Good morning sex... oh bae, you good? You look rough this morning."

I looked in the mirror and tried to straighten myself up.

"I'll be fine. My nerves are still getting the best of me, and I just found Kim's ass in the bathroom with Sean. They said they were smoking. Like, when did she start smoking?" I asked, all worked up.

BREANNA J.

Keyz started to laugh.

"That nigga," Keyz said, still laughing.

"Keyz, it's not funny," I said, getting a little mad.

"Bae, don't let these grown muthafuckers get you all worked up. Come here and let me help you feel better," he said as he pulled me into his arms.

He kissed me on the forehead and then lifted my chin to kiss me on the lips.

"Baby, this weekend is all yours. Fuck what everyone else is doing," he said to me in a calming way.

Keyz scooped me up and put me on the bed.

"Want me to make you feel better?" he asked with a smirk.

"Yeah, I guess," I said with a devilish look on my face. "But let's wait until after breakfast," I said to him.

"Fuck breakfast, I got food right here," he said as he started to undress me.

In The Name of Love

Chapter Twenty-Two

Me and Keyz had a moment together and joined everyone else for breakfast or what was left of it. Once everything was gone and cleaned up, I reminded Keyz about the wedding rehearsal and dinner tonight at 6 P.M. He assured me he wouldn't forget or be late and departed.

Me and the girls started on our day as well. We went down to the spa that the hotel had.   We started with pedicures and manicures. We talked about men, sex and other things that brought us laughter. After the pedicures and manicures, we decide to do a little shopping before facials and massages.

Katrina and Tasha ran off in search of bathing suits for a party they heard was happening at the hotel tonight. Me and Kim looked for some stuff to bring home with us. We found matching sundresses and brought a bunch of different outfits just in case we didn't like something we brought to wear on the trip.

While Kim was trying on a dress in the fitting room, my phone rang.

"Hello," I answered.

"Sasha, I am sorry to call you while you're on your trip but…" Tony began.

"Tony, if this is something about us being together, it's not going to happen! I am here and a day away from marrying

BREANNA J.

Keyz."

"No Sasha, it actually has nothing to do with that it."

I cut him off.

"Then, whatever it is it can wait until I return home. I don't want to hear it or deal with it. Have a good day," I said, ending the call.

I hung up.

Not today, not before my wedding.

Nothing was going to take away my happiness.

Kim walked out of the dressing room.

"What do you think?" she questioned as she spun around.

"It's nice," I told her.

"What's wrong, Sasha? You seem distracted," she said.

"I'm good," I told her as I started walking towards Katrina and Tasha.

They were coming our way.

"Y'all ready for lunch?" I asked them as we all met up.

"Yeah, we are ready, but first you need to take this," Katrina said as she took a pregnancy test out her purse.

In The Name of Love

I laughed it off.

"Girl, I'm not pregnant! Put that away."

All three girls looked at me.

"Sasha, if you're not pregnant then just take the test and get the question out of the air. And we can laugh about it later," Kim said.

"But I know I'm not," I pleaded to them, trying to convince myself just as well.

"Can you just pee on the stick so we can go and eat?"

Katrina pushed the test towards me.

I snatched the test from her and went into the restroom. I sat there for a minute before taking the test.

"Well, here goes nothing," I said to myself as I took the stick and peed on.

I came out the restroom not sure of what the results were going to tell.

"Where is the test at?" Kim asked.

"Right here," I said, opening the paper towels I had it wrapped in.

"Well, did you look and see what it say?" Katrina asked.

BREANNA J.

"No, I can't look at it," I said to the girls.

"Oh, so now Ms. I'm not Pregnant wants to be scared. Give it here," Kim said laughing as she snatched the used test out of my hand.

"That's the side I peed on that your holding with your hand, smart ass!" I barked at her.

She fumbled the stick and dropped it on the floor in the store. We all circled around the stick. We all looked at the test in shock.

"Is that two lines?" Kim asked.

"It sure looks like it," Katrina said.

Tasha took the paper towel out my hands and bent over to pick up the test.

"Well Sasha girl…" she said with a long dramatic pause. "Girl, you're pregnant… congrats!"

The girls hugged me, but I stood there emotionless.

I'm carrying a child, this can't be true. I thought to myself.

So many thoughts crossed my mind, but the biggest question was how the hell was I supposed to tell Keyz.

In The Name of Love

Chapter Twenty-Three

For the rest of the night, I was so not myself. I made the girls promise not to bring up the pregnancy test in front of Keyz. I wanted to tell him on my own time in my own way. When the rehearsal dinner was over, me and Keyz had out last unmarried kiss and said our see you later's.

I would be staying in our room for the night and Keyz would be stay in the room with Sean for the night. It was basically the only traditional thing we were doing for this whole wedding. That night, I could not sleep. I was like a child the night before the first day of school. I tossed and turned all night.

Finally, I got up and grabbed a notebook from my purse and went on the balcony.

As I sat there waiting for the sun to come up, I wrote a letter to Keyz for him to read before the wedding.

To my lover, my friend, my protector and my husband

Our day is finally here. The beginning of a new chapter for us two. Today when we stand in front of God and our friends please know that this is not a show to me. I am promising to give you my unconditional love, my fullest devotion and all the tender loving care I have in me. I promise my faithfulness and loyalty to you and you alone for the rest of our lives. I promise to commit me and my sanity to you. I will always be your main support and your biggest fan. I will pledge to you respect and to always let you be the man and king. I will let

Breanna J.

you play your role and never make you feel less of a man. I will be your strength when your weakness. An ear when you just need to be heard. I promise all this to you today with hopes that you are nothing less than the man I know you can be.

Thank you for choosing me when you could have had anyone else. Thank you for being everything I needed and more at the times that I needed you the most. No matter what good or bad we may have faced or will face I know God has us and our union, because he made me just for you and you just for me. And for that I praise and thank him.

From today forward we combine as one. To always walk together in spirit and in truth. Today I give you my heart, my life and love; in exchange for your last night. And in nine months we will give each the best joy of all.

I love you, Sasha

I went back inside. It was still early and everyone was still sleeping. Seeing that I had time to waste because the wedding wasn't until sunset; I took a shower and got dressed.

I went and walked the beach. I walked the beach and thought about everything the led me to this day. I knew my mom and brother had to be up in heaven smiling down on me. I had made it through hurt, betrayal, and tears and found love. I had found someone that sacrificed for me and promised me a forever. Keyz was not perfect, but neither was I. We were perfect for each other.

IN THE NAME OF LOVE

I headed back to the hotel. I stopped by the gift shop in the hotel lobby and grabbed a ginger ale and another pregnancy test just to be sure.

When I got back to the suite, the guys were in the room making noise and only Katrina was out in the living room. She was drinking coffee and staring out the sliding double doors in a daze.

"Good morning" I said to her.

She turned and smiled.

"Good morning, are you ready for today?"

I shook my hands, letting her know I was so-so.

She stood up and walked over to the table I was standing near.

"What you got in the bag?" she asked.

"Dang nosy," I said to her, laughing.

Katrina laughed too and as we stood there, Kim came out her room.

"What's so funny?" she asked.

"Y'all come with me in my room," I said.

We walked in my room.

BREANNA J.

I took out like pregnancy test and showed it to the girls.

"I just need to be sure before I tell Keyz," I told them.

"Okay, well go ahead. We'll be out here waiting," Katrina said.

I walked in the bathroom and sat on the toilet. It seemed as if because I knew I had to pee on this stick, nothing wanted to come out.

After a few minutes Kim yelled through the door, "Did you go yet?"

"No, I can't!" I answered back to her.

"Turn on some water," she suggested.

I leaned over from the toilet and turned the sink on. It must go been a mental thing because once the water was on, I started to pee. I finished up and put the test on a piece of tissue on the corner while I washed my hands and opened the door.

"Now, we wait," I said to the girls.as we sat in the room waiting.

I heard the guys come out their room talking and laughing and then I heard a door close.

After a while, Katrina looked at me.

"You ready?" she asked me.

In The Name of Love

I got up and walked in the bathroom. They followed. We all looked at the test sitting the sink's counter.

I started to cry.

"I'm pregnant, I am really pregnant," I said.

Kim and Katrina smiled and started to chant, "You're going to be a mommy, you're going to be a mommy."

I smiled and walked out the bathroom.

"I want to tell Keyz," I said.

Kim burst out with, "But you're not supposed to see each other."

I looked around the room thinking of how I could tell him. Then, I notice that Keyz left his shoes for the wedding under the bed.

I pulled out the shoebox.

"Look, he left his shoes so we can put the test and the letter I wrote him in the shoe box on top. One of you can take it across the hall," I said to the girls.

"Good idea, and I got a gift box that my watch came in that we can put the test in," Kim said all excited.

She ran out the room to get the box. I folded the letter and stuck it in the box. When Kim came back, I put the test in the gift box she had.

BREANNA J.

"Katrina, you take it," I said.

"Why can't I take it, Sash'?" Kim asked.

"Sit your hot ass down. You just want to see Sean," Katrina said.

"I mean I'm not saying yes or no, but either way, the boy is fine," Kim said.

We all laughed.

"Kim, he is fine and old. Get you someone your age. Go ahead, Katrina," I said.

Katrina walked out the room and I watched her walk across the living room and knock on Sean's room door.

Sean came to the door.

"Give this to Keyz," she told him.

Katrina came back in the room and before we could spark a conversation we heard Keyz scream out, "YO!!!" and then it sounded like a stampede coming towards the room door.

Keyz swung the door open and charged towards me. Once he was close enough, he picked me up off my feet and spun me around the room.

He was hugging me and screaming, "We having a baby!"

IN THE NAME OF LOVE

Kim yelled out, "Keyz, you are not supposed to be in here!"

Keyz brushed her off, "Fuck that, we having a baby, y'all!"

We all laughed.

Sean and Tasha was now standing in the door way laughing and smiling with the rest of us. The fact that Keyz was so excited about the news made me that much more happy about the happy.

When Keyz finally let me go, Katrina kicked them out.

"Get out, we got to get her ready," she said.

Once the guys were out, the glam began. Tasha came in there with a bomb wig she had made just for me. Kim brought my wedding dress over from her room and hung it up .Katrina started to set up all her makeup. They all helped get me get ready.

Before I knew it, it was time for us to go down and prepare for the wedding to start. As we got to the elevator, I looked at my girls. They looked so lovely and they were here to support me.

When we got downstairs, the wedding planner met us in waiting room.

"Okay ladies, its time. The men are in their places and it's

BREANNA J.

your turn to walk down," she said joyfully.

"Ladies, bring it in. Before we walk out of here, I want to thank you. Thank y'all for going through the ups and down with me and Keyz. Thank you for leaving the grind to come on this trip with me, and most of all thank you for making me look so beautiful today," I said as we had a group hug.

We all wiped our faces and tired not to mess up our make-up.

The wedding planner handed Tasha and Katrina their flowers and they walked out. Shortly after, I heard the music start to play.

Kim and I stood there looking for each other. Then Kim reached out for my veil and as she covered me with it she said, "Good bye Ms. Brown."

She turned to the wedding planner, grabbed her flowers and walked out.

Then the moment had come. I was all alone. I grabbed my bouquet and stood in front of the doors.

When they finally opened, I looked around and scanned the beach and the beautiful view. The sight that brought tears to my eyes was Keyz standing at the altar crying and waiting for me.

As I walked down the aisle, I had flashback of the good and the bad. I saw Keyz and CJ chilling at my dining

IN THE NAME OF LOVE

room table, smiling and laughing while I cooked for them. I saw my mom before the drugs. I saw the night I hit Simone with my gun. I saw the moment I met Kim.

By the time Keyz lifted my veil, I had tears rolling down my face.

He wiped my tears.

"Hey there, beautiful"

I smiled at him.

He grabbed my hand and we turned towards the preacher and he started.

BREANNA J.

Chapter Twenty-Four

The wedding ceremony was amazing. I married the person that I couldn't be without in front of the people the meant the most to us, but the honeymoon was even better. I thought that we were going back to the suite to spend our honeymoon with our friends, but Keyz had another suite set up already just for us so that we can share time as newly-weds.

This trip was everything I could have ever wished for and more. But, now, it was time to head home and get back to reality.

As I stood in the mirror in the bathroom looking at myself I couldn't believe how much this trip had changed me. I came here as Sasha Brown the girlfriend of Kendrick and salon owner. I was leaving as Mrs. Sasha Shaw "the wife" of Kendrick Shaw, and the mother of his unborn child and the successful salon owner.

Keyz came in the bathroom.

"Bae, you ready to go?"

I smiled at him.

"Yes, let's go home."

He reached out his hand and grabbed mine. Down to the lobby we headed to meet everyone else. The gang was waiting down there for us. As we all loaded up into the van to the

In The Name of Love

airport, I couldn't help but to notice that Kim was extremely into her phone.

Once everyone was in the van, I asked, "Kim, you good?"

She nodded her head while still looking down at her phone.

"Kim… Kim!" I said.

She finally looked up at me. "What's going on with you? Why are you so into your phone?" I asked.

She looked at me and then looked around to everyone else in the van. No one was paying us any attention. They all had headphones in and were in their own world.

"It's Simone; before we came here I had finally heard from her. She had texted me and said she was going to Puerto Rico to see her parents. Now, all morning she's been texting me off the wall shit like she's back home but she's going to be going away again and that she will hit me when she can, and then when I find out what she did not to look at her differently.

I looked at Kim.

"I told you don't get your feeling wrapped up in that girl, Now, look at you."

Kim gave me a side eye.

"Sasha, this is not the time for the I told you so. I know

BREANNA J.

you don't like her because the history, but I think she's in real trouble."

I looked at Kim and put my headphones in. I closed my eyes and waited to arrive at the airport.

Once we got to the airport, we had just enough time to check our bags, go through security and board the plane. As we boarded the plane, a call came through on my cell.

"Hello?" I answered.

"Sasha, don't hang up! This is important. Tell Keyz not to…" I hung up.

Not today, Tony.

I got on the plane and sat next to Keyz.

"Are you ready to return home as a married man Mr. Shaw?" I asked him.

"Yes I am, Mrs. Shaw," he said as he gave me a kiss.

I looked down the row to try to see if I could see Kim. Her head was still down so I assumed she was still in her phone. I couldn't help but think that everything we had built was going to go downhill all over Kim's feelings. Regardless, I cared about Kim so if this girl's well-being meant that much to her, when we got home, I would help her make sure she was okay. I mean, that was what family did.

IN THE NAME OF LOVE

Chapter Twenty-Five

The flight home seemed to go by way faster than the flight there, but I couldn't lie. As I unboarded this plane, I couldn't be happier to be home. We all grabbed our bags and headed outside to go to our cars.

I said my goodbye to Katrina and Tasha and they walked off.

Keyz was talking to Sean, so I made my way to Kim.

"When you get home and get settled in call me, I got some people we can use to find her."

Kim looked at me and smiled, "Thanks for being the bigger person."

As I turned around, I saw two cops walking up on Keyz and Sean.

"Kendrick Shaw?" one of the cops asked.

"Yeah, that's me," Keyz answered back.

The cop pulled his hand cuffs out.

"Kendrick Shaw, you are under arrest."

I rushed over to them.

"Excuse me, what the hell is going on here? Why is my

BREANNA J.

husband in handcuffs?" I asked.

"Ma'am, please back up."

By this time, Sean was flipping out and the cops were threating to arrest him, too.

"Kendrick Shaw, you are under arrest for the murder of Calvin Brown Jr." the cop finally said.

My heart hit my feet as I let out a scream. Kim came to comfort me.

As they dragged Keyz off, he looked at me with a look I couldn't explain. Once they had him in the cop car, the cops came back over to me.

"Ma'am, can I ask you to come down to the police station with us?"

I looked at the guy and rolled my eyes.

"I am going with her, I'm her sister," Kim yelled out.

The police officer walked me over to another car they had waiting and put me in the back seat. Kim got in on the other side.

As we rode to the police station, the words kept replaying in my ear.

"Kendrick Shaw, you are under arrest for the murder of Calvin Brown Jr."

In The Name of Love

How could my husband kill my brother and I not know? How could I have been laying in a bed and loving on a man that took the purest love I know away from me?

As we arrived in front of the police station, Kim grabbed my hand.

I looked her in the eye.

"We got this," Kim said to me.

I stepped out the car and walked into the police station.

"Sasha," a voice said from behind me.

I turned around to Tony walking towards me. He hugged me.

I looked at him, confused.

"Tony, what the fuck is going on here? This better not be some shit that you put together," I said to him.

Tony pulled me off to the side.

"This has nothing to do with me. I tried to warn you when I called you. They have a witness that calming she and Keyz partnered together to kill your brother."

Before I could say anything, a cop came over.

"Sasha Brown?" he asked.

BREANNA J.

"It's Shaw." I replied as I turned to him.

He extended his hand.

"I am Officer Murry," I looked at his hand.

"Can I ask you to follow me?"

I walked behind him and Kim followed behind me.

"What is going on here and when can I see my husband? There has to be some misunderstanding here."

Office Murry said nothing.

He walked me into a room with a large window and pulled up the shade.

"Do you know this woman?" he asked

"Simone!" Kim yelled out.

Officer Murry and I both looked at her.

"Yes, I know her. She was my husband's mistress and she is a friend to my sister. Why does she matter?"

"Mrs. Shaw, please take a seat," he said with one arm extended towards the table in the room and the other closing the shade back. We sat down.

Once the officer sat across the table from us, I grabbed Kim's hand under the table.

IN THE NAME OF LOVE

"Mrs. Shaw, that woman in there came into our station hours ago claiming that she had been sleeping with your husband for a year and was pregnant with his child. She also told us that before all this happen herself and your husband set up your brother Calvin Jr., who was at that time Simone's boyfriend, to be murdered. Now, do you know why she would say all that?"

I shook my head no.

"How do you guys even know what she's saying is true?" I asked.

"Well, the story she told us about the murder matched perfectly to the evidence we collected at the time of the murder. She told us that she and Calvin had ventured out to a park in the middle of the night. She said that she bent down to please him sexually and the shooter, your husband, shot Calvin through the passenger's side door. She also told us where to find the gun Kendrick used to shoot him. When we went searching for it, we found in the wall of one of the rental properties you guys owned, just like she said we would," the cop said.

As the cop spoke my stomach begann to feel tighter and tighter.

I got up from the table holding my stomach and trying to walk towards the door.

"Sasha, you okay?" Kim asked.

I couldn't answer. I felt my body grow weak and the room

BREANNA J.

starting to spin.

Kim jumped out her chair to grab me and Officer Murry rushed over to aid her.

"Call someone, she's pregnant!" I could hear Kim yell to the officer.

I saw her crying before my eyes closed.

In The Name of Love

To Be Continued...

BREANNA J.

CPSIA information can be obtained
at www.ICGtesting.com
Printed in the USA
LVOW10s1728130318
569703LV00017B/1025/P